FH

REVENGE BY FIRE

Bill Williams

Steve Ross stops struggling to run his small ranch during Arizona's worst drought in living memory. But despite his intention of leaving town, he's suddenly forced to either hang for murder, or become the Deputy Marshal of Craigy Plains. Ross, never having fired a pistol, is appointed as lawman and taught how to handle a weapon. But it's not long before he's severely tested — drawn into tragic events that put his own life in the greatest danger.

THE STAKED PLAINS

Billy Moore

Buffalo-hide hunter Quentin McLeod rescues Carlotta Mainord from Comanche raiders, only for them both to face further hostility from the Indians, flash floods and white brigands. Later, arriving in New Mexico, they think they're safe — but there's even greater danger. Carlotta Mainord is attacked and left helpless in a coma, then McLeod is blamed and accused of being a Comanchero. Can he convince the hanging jury of his innocence, and will he escape the lynch mob in time?

LANIGAN AND THE SHE-WOLF

Silas Cutler hires Shawnee Lanigan to track down the bank robbers who abducted his eighteen-year-old daughter, Sara Beth. The ruthless 'La Loba' leads the all female gang. When he tracks the outlaws down, he's staggered to discover the real reason for the kidnapping . . . Forced to report his failed rescue mission, he takes work supervising security for a mining operation. Lanigan unveils a plot and ultimately faces a vengeful mob — aware that they can't all make it out alive . . .

Books by Ronald Martin Wade
in the Linford Western Library:

LANIGAN AND THE
SILENT MOURNER

RONALD MARTIN WADE

LANIGAN AND THE SHE-WOLF

Complete and Unabridged

LINFORD
Leicester

First published in Great Britain in 2009 by
Robert Hale Limited
London

First Linford Edition
published 2011
by arrangement with
Robert Hale Limited
London

British Library CIP Data

Wade, Ronald Martin.
  Lanigan and the She-Wolf. - -
  (Linford western library)
  1. Western stories.
  2. Large type books.
  I. Title I. Series
  823.9'2–dc22

ISBN 978–1–44480–515–4

Published by
F. A. Thorpe (Publishing)
Anstey, Leicestershire

Set by Words & Graphics Ltd.
Anstey, Leicestershire
Printed and bound in Great Britain by
T. J. International Ltd., Padstow, Cornwall

This book is printed on acid-free paper

1

It was a cool March afternoon in Sidelia, county seat of Masters County, Texas. The sky was clear and the Sidelians were going about their business as usual. Rufus Woodrow, unshaved, unbathed and with an aching head, sat on the edge of the boardwalk in front of the saddle shop. Dick Helms, the bartender at the Pecos Belle Saloon, would no longer let him sit in front of his establishment, claiming it was bad for business for patrons to walk past a stinking drunk on the way in.

Rufus was dead broke and was wondering where he could cadge a drink when he saw seven riders walking their horses into town and up the main street. This, in itself, was not unusual. There were always riders in Sidelia, either locals or drovers passing by with a herd and coming into town for supplies or, more likely, a drink of whiskey. They looked different to Rufus, but his thoughts were too confused to nail it down.

The riders had obviously been on the trail for a while. The dusters they wore were coated with grime, their faces smudged with trail dust. They hunched in their saddles wearily, faces down, hidden behind the brims of their hats.

Three of them reined to a stop in front of the Sidelia Bank, slowly dismounted, tied their horses and casually strolled inside. Another one tied up his horse two doors down and stood on the boardwalk, looking up and down the street. The remaining three continued on down the street until Rufus lost sight of them. Rufus didn't recognize any of the riders and reasoned that they were strangers. Consequently, it was logical for him to assume they wouldn't know him and might be susceptible to a hard luck story.

A well-dressed lady emerged from

the bank door, putting something into her purse. Rufus recognized her as Mrs Logan, wife of the Baptist minister. He turned away so as not to be recognized.

After Mrs Logan disappeared and he was no longer in danger of a stern lecture, Rufus pulled himself to his feet and limped across the dusty street to where the stranger stood on the boardwalk. As he approached, he noticed that the rider appeared to be a big man with a lantern jaw. Rufus hesitated for a few moments, then screwed up his courage and approached him with the plea he had been using since Lee surrendered twenty years before.

'Pardon me, sir,' he said, hesitantly. 'Could you help a poor wounded war veteran? I haven't been able to work for six months and I need a meal.'

The rider turned and looked at Rufus with hard eyes. Those flat, steely eyes frightened Rufus and he took a step back, his own eyes wide.

The rider stared for a moment then

smiled a thin smile, handed Rufus a coin and brushed past him, walking purposely toward the bank. Rufus examined the coin and determined it was a whole dollar. He turned and called after the stranger, 'Thanks, mister, God bless you'.

Without turning, the stranger raised a hand and waved an acknowledgement just before going into the bank.

Rufus could already taste the soothing balm. He felt the warmness in his stomach, creeping up his throat to his head, the lightness in his brain, the bearing away of all pain.

At that moment, there were gunshots! The sounds of the shots were varied, like it was a big gunfight. It was happening at the other end of the street! Rufus stepped into the street and peered down its length. Other citizens were doing the same, curious and seemingly oblivious to the danger of a stray bullet. The town marshal and his deputy emerged from the marshal's office. Both pulled their weapons and ran toward the disturbance.

Rufus, remembering his new treasure, lost interest in the shooting and headed toward the Prairie Flower Saloon, but saw something from the corner of his eye. Four figures in dusters were backing out of the front door, their pistols drawn, held waist-high and aimed at the bank's interior. Two of them held canvas bags. One of the four was the big fellow who had given Rufus his dollar. The big man turned and hurried toward Rufus. Rufus stood transfixed.

Mounting their horses, the other three galloped away, back the way they'd come. Rufus' benefactor hurried by him, mounted up and started after the other three at a lope. But then the horse veered toward the side of the street where a young lady was watching. To Rufus' surprise, the big rider leaned from the saddle and seized the girl around the waist, pulled her up onto the horse then spurred it to a gallop. The girl screamed and her arms and legs flailed as she struggled with her captor. She was still struggling when the horse disappeared from sight.

Shaken, Rufus headed toward the Prairie Flower for something to soothe his nerves and perhaps to cadge a few more drinks with his tale.

★   ★   ★

Shawnee Lanigan was sound asleep and dreaming of green fields sprinkled with bluebonnets and Indian paintbrush cooled by a gentle breeze from the southeast, when something intruded upon his dream, perhaps a gathering storm; he heard thunder in the distance. That's when he was awakened by violent shaking and an urgent voice whispering frantically, 'It's my husband! He's looking for me.'

Shawnee came awake and looked at the dark-haired woman who had just roused him. He heard doors slamming somewhere down the hotel hallway and a voice roaring, 'Mildred! Where in hell are you? I'm gonna whup your ass and shoot that son-of-a-bitch you're with.'

Shawnee was wide-awake at that point and acutely aware that his own pistol was back at his rooming house. While Mildred was doing her best to wiggle into her clothes, Shawnee sprang from the bed, grabbed his hat and jammed it on his head, picked up his clothes with one hand and his boots with the other and headed for the window. He stuck his head out the window and belatedly remembered that they were in a second-story room overlooking the alley.

There was a crash as the husband ripped open the door of the next-door room. The noise gave wings to Shawnee's feet. He tossed the clothes and boots through the window, clambered over the sill and hung by his fingertips momentarily, then let go. He fell into the shrubbery under the window, hollering as the small branches seemed to flay the flesh from his legs and backside. Despite what felt like serious wounds, he sprang clear of the hedge, gathered up his belongings and fled at a dead run down the alley.

As he ran, he met two young Latinas carrying laundry baskets. '*Que un palo!*' one of them cried delightedly.

'Can't stop right now, ladies,' he said as he ran past them. As he dodged into the open door of a shed, he heard the girls laughing.

Shawnee pulled on his clothes, leaned against a wall to put on his boots, and continued on down the alley with frequent backward glances. He arrived at his rooming house in short order and went directly to his room. He rummaged around in his war bag for a moment till he came up with 'Doctor Miracle's Udder Cream' and pulled the top off the can. Shedding his clothes, he smeared the cream on all the places scratched raw by the bushes. The udder cream was the most effective medication he knew of and he had used it for years on nearly every blemish or wound short of those made by knife or gunshot.

He gingerly pulled on his underwear and lay across the bed. He decided he had enjoyed enough excitement for one day and would spend the rest of the day in meditation. It was not to be, however; there was a knock at his door and a voice asking, 'Shawnee, you in there?'

'Oh, hell's kitchen!' Shawnee exclaimed, painfully getting out of the bed. Certain muscles were getting stiff from the fall he had taken. He opened the door to Oscar Watts, deputy sheriff, Rio County.

Watts grinned broadly and said, 'You are here! Boy hidy, I didn't expect that.'

'What do you want, Watts?' Shawnee growled, turning back to the bed.

'What on earth happened to your legs and back, Shawnee?' the deputy asked, somewhat amazed.

'I asked you first,' Shawnee said, frowning.

'Oh!' Watts exclaimed, suddenly remembering. 'Sheriff Horn needs to talk with you.'

'Bout what?'

'Danged if I know. A letter come a little while ago and the sheriff read it and told me, 'Go find Shawnee and tell him I need to see 'im.' He didn't give me no reason.'

Shawnee scratched his head with both hands and said, 'Oh hell, I might as well go on and talk to the old fart. It may involve a job and come to think of it, it might be wise to be out of town for a few days.'

'Your turn,' Watts said.

'What?'

'Your turn to answer my question. I answered yours, now it's your turn. What happened to your back and legs?'

Shawnee looked disgusted. 'I got tangled up with a girl that keeps her fingernails too long,' he muttered.

'Damn!' Watts exclaimed. He thought for a moment, then asked with a wicked grin, 'Was it fun?'

★　★　★

Sheriff Horn was an old friend in the sense that he didn't beat the hell out of Shawnee every time he got drunk and had to be locked up. Sheriff Horn knew Shawnee's talents as well as his shortcomings and knew the 'quarter-Injun' wastrel could be counted on in a tight spot.

'Shawnee,' the sheriff said, waving a letter at him, 'when in hell are you going to get an address so these people that want to get hold of you know where to find you. I get a letter addressed to me and open it up and there's another one to you inside. I'm fed up with being your personal post office.'

'You know I really appreciate that, too, Sheriff,' Shawnee said, ingratiatingly. 'You've been as good as gold 'bout that. I don't know what I'd do without you.'

'Put that snake oil back in the bottle, Shawnee. From now on, you can get your mail general delivery just like any other homeless person.'

'Aw shucks, Sheriff,' Shawnee whined. 'Getting my mail at General Delivery just doesn't carry the same *cachet* as it does going to you.'

Sheriff Horn frowned. 'Cash shay? What in hell is that? Sounds French,' he said suspiciously.

'It means that me receiving my mail at your office makes me look on the up and up,' Shawnee explained.

'Or that you have a permanent room in my gaol,' the sheriff snorted. 'Here!' he added, tossing the letter to Shawnee.

Shawnee sat gingerly in the lone visitor's chair, and finally found a part of his backside he could put his weight on. He tilted his hat back on his head and tore open the letter. He read over it quickly, looked up at the sheriff who was waiting for a comment, and reread the letter.

The sheriff finally asked impatiently, 'Who is it from, Shawnee, somebody who needs your help or wants you dead?'

Shawnee said, 'It's from a fellow up

in Pyote by the name of Cutler. Seems that a gang of bank-robbers carried off his daughter. Listen to this:

'*Dear Mister Lanigan,*

'*I am sending you this letter out of desperation since the law has been unable to help me.*

'*Three weeks ago, my daughter Sara Beth was taken by a gang of bank robbers during a holdup of the Sidelia Bank. She was in Sidelia shopping for piece goods when the holdup occurred. The robbers shot down two people and during their escape, the leader rode up to my daughter, who was transfixed with fear, leaned out of the saddle, seized her and rode off with the gang while my daughter cried piteously for help.*

'*The law has searched, or at least they say they have, but have turned up no trace of Sara Beth or the gang. A Texas Ranger came by a week ago and gave me no encouragement. Therefore, I must turn to you. I understand you are a tracker that has had reasonable success in apprehending criminals or sending them to face their maker. I am calling upon you to help me in this time of need.*

'*I am not a wealthy man but I am not badly off and I will give my worldly wealth for the safe return of my daughter.*

'Hoping for an encouraging answer, I remain

'*Sincerely yours,*

'*Silas Cutler.*'

'Well Shawnee,' Horn said, 'sounds like a job just made in heaven for you.'

'You know, Emory,' Shawnee replied. 'I never know whether they are made in heaven or in hell. Most of the time, you can't tell the difference.'

'You got money to get you to Pyote?' Sheriff Horn asked. 'Usually by now, you've given all your money to the girls at the Garden of Earthly Delights.'

'This time I haven't,' Shawnee answered, smiling. 'I ain't been home long enough to spend it all.'

'Or lose it to those scruffy bums you play poker with?'

Shawnee smiled. 'They aren't really bums, they just lack certain social graces.'

'You talking about Bum McReedy, Wall-Eye Brewster and Trace Chain Stokes lacking social graces? That's like saying Abe Lincoln was a Yankee.'

Shawnee chuckled. 'You know, I think why I lose so much to those fellows is I can't read Brewster. He puts me off my game.'

'How's that?'

'It's that left eye of his, always staring to his left. I can't tell whether he's playing his own hand or the one held by the fellow next to him.'

★ ★ ★

Shawnee's time on the trail wasn't pleasant for two reasons: because of the injuries to his backside, and the voices. He found that bandaging up the worst scrapings after applying ample amounts of udder cream helped enormously, but when he climbed into his bedroll at night, the voices started up again, first murmuring and then getting louder. When the old shaman started in on him, he yelled, 'Shut up, you old bastard!' The voices trailed off after that.

He spent a week on the trail getting to Pecos, which was the biggest town anywhere near Pyote. There was no rail service to or from Rio County, so he had to hit the trail. His only companions were his paint mare, Candy, and Pizzaro, the burro who carried the supplies needed for survival on the trail.

Candy was another Shawnee Lanigan departure from conventional wisdom. The horses used on a drive or other working trip were invariably geldings. But, years before, when Shawnee had returned a runaway daughter to a poor but decent family, they had no cash for his fee so they offered the mare instead. Shawnee didn't really need a mare but he decided that under the circumstances, it was a fair trade. By the time he had tracked down the daughter and the ne'er-do-well with whom she had run away for a life of romance and adventure, the lover, with threats and generous use of his fists, was trying to force the girl into a brothel to earn a living for both of them. Highly offended, Shawnee beat the ingrate senseless and the grateful girl gladly accompanied him back to the bosom of her family.

When Shawnee arrived in Pecos, he thanked his lucky stars there was a hotel with twelve rooms and a staff who knew what a bathtub was. Shawnee put up Candy and Pizzaro in the stable, made certain they had a stall with clean hay and plenty of oats, then saw to himself. After scraping off a week's worth of west Texas trail dust and shaving, he looked admiringly at himself in the mirror and was satisfied with what he saw.

Going downstairs to the lobby of Pecos' only hotel, he inquired where a gentleman might quench a mighty thirst and was directed to Pecos Bill's saloon half a block down.

Walking into Pecos Bill's was a pleasant experience. The aroma of beer, cigar smoke and whiskey made him feel at home. The piano player was in good form and was tinkling out the most popular melodies on a piano that was only slightly out of tune. Shawnee strode to the bar, ordered a whiskey with a beer chaser and looked around the room in the way of orientation. The quality of the whiskey was on a par with that poured across the west; if it made a man gasp for breath while his eyes watered, he considered it to have been distilled with the proper authority and therefore worth the ten cents that one paid for it.

'Gimmee another shot of this tarantula juice, professor,' Shawnee rasped, his eyes watering. 'How do you make this stuff so smooth?'

The bartender, who wore a spectacular and heavily waxed mustache, smiled as he poured another shot. 'We add at least a half-dozen rattlesnake heads to each barrel; it takes the rough edges off.'

After two shots of Pecos Bill's finest, washed down with a beer that was at least cool and wet, Shawnee felt that familiar glow that started in his stomach and spread up his gullet to a point behind his eyes. Between the piano player's efforts and the whiskey glow, the voices faded into the background. He was just beginning to feel that something was missing, when suddenly, there it was: perfume! Cheap, pervasive and intoxicating perfume enveloped him. Shawnee turned and there she was, a young, dark-eyed, raven-haired woman with just the right amount of plumpness that inspired admiration in climes south of the border: a predilection that Shawnee shared. Her white blouse was wide-necked and exposed an interesting expanse of firm brown flesh and when she stood close, or bent forward, the admiring bystander was treated to a glimpse of inviting, well-rounded breasts. The predatory female allowed the poor weak male to feast his eyes on her charms until he suffered a weakening of even the strongest resolve. She then administered the *coup de grâce*, the warm and soft, but inexorable, pressure of a full breast against his elbow.

The next morning, after congratulating himself on not being robbed by his inamorata-for-hire, having breakfasted on eggs, bacon, flap jacks and black strap molasses, Shawnee roused Candy from her comfortable stall and they made the short trip to Pyote for a rendezvous with fate or, as Shawnee preferred to say, a paying customer.

The Cutler home was neat, with a Spartan, but carefully tended yard. The house itself was spacious and simply appointed. Shawnee noticed that, in all the windows he could see, the window shades were pulled to a uniform length. A modestly attired, pretty girl of about fifteen years answered Shawnee's knock. She introduced herself as Mary

Jane, took his hat and ushered him into the parlour.

Silas Cutler was not what Shawnee expected. He had expected to see a dishevelled, grieving father, gaunt from lack of sleep and concern for his child. But Silas Cutler more closely resembled a Baptist deacon in search of a backslider. His face was spare, stern and clean-shaven. The cheekbones stood out and his thin lips covered his teeth with difficulty. The result was a forbidding countenance that seemed to disapprove of everything his piercing blue eyes beheld.

Mary Jane introduced Shawnee and promptly withdrew.

'Would you care for some refreshment after your journey, Mister Lanigan?' Cutler asked, waving toward a chair. 'Perhaps a glass of water or fresh milk?'

'Nothing, thank you,' Shawnee replied.

Cutler sat facing Shawnee with a stiff posture, hands on the arms of his chair, knees together. 'Then we will get down to business,' he said. 'Thank you for coming so promptly.'

Shawnee nodded acknowledgment and leaned forward to hear what Cutler had to say.

'As I told you in my letter,' the black-clad man went on, 'Sara Beth, my eldest, was taken off the street by an outlaw. Since I have received no ransom demands, I assume the outlaws intend to keep her for purposes known only to themselves and Satan. I cannot tell you, Mister Lanigan, how we have suffered at the uncertainty of her fate. Since her mother's death some years ago, I have striven to raise her and her two sisters up in the path of righteousness and to disdain the baser nature of most of the people who infest this part of the world. I have taught her to keep herself pure before the Almighty until a worthy husband could ask for her hand.' Cutler gripped the arms of the chair in which he sat until his knuckles turned white. 'I assure you, Mister Lanigan,' he went on between clenched teeth, 'it is better that she be dead in an unmarked grave than ill-used by those Godless monsters.'

'I understand, sir,' Shawnee replied. Slightly taken aback by the turn of the old man's emotions, he changed the subject. 'How much do you know about the gang that took her?'

'Very little,' Cutler replied. 'The law in Sidelia may know something, not that it has helped that, er, group.'

Shawnee had the impression that an epithet of some kind had almost escaped Cutler's lips. 'Was it a known gang?' he asked.

'Yes, the local law seemed to have some idea of who they were. They called the leader 'La Loba'.'

Shawnee wasn't sure he'd heard properly. He started to ask the name again but knew he could get a more accurate reading from Sidelia's peace officers.

'What does Sara Beth look like?'

Cutler put the fingertips of his hands together and stared somewhere over Shawnee's head while he visualized her. 'She is eighteen years old, has long, dark brown hair, blue eyes. She's about five feet four inches tall, neither thin nor fat. Mary Jane, who met you at the door, looks like a younger version of her.'

'Do you have a picture of her?'

'Yes, I thought you might need one. I have it here,' Cutler replied, handing a small frame to Shawnee without looking at the photograph it contained.

Sara Beth was indeed an older version of Mary Jane; her attractive face a portrait of innocence. She wore a high collared, dark dress for the portrait. Shawnee felt uneasy in his stomach knowing how a group of amoral degenerates might abuse such an innocent.

'Besides returning your daughter to you, what else do you want me to do?' Shawnee asked.

'You can send the villain that took her to stand before the highest judge,' Cutler replied in a sepulchral tone.

'Chances are, sir,' Shawnee said softly, 'if I bring your daughter back alive, I will have to do that anyway. Then on the other hand, I may end up standing before that judge myself.'

'Yours is a dangerous line of work,' the old man stated unemotionally.

'Yes sir, it is. That's why I ask for high fees. There're not many around to compete with me.'

'What do you charge?'

Shawnee replied, 'Well, sir. It depends on how long it takes and how many men I have to kill. Then there's the possibility I may lean into a bullet or two and keep walking. I add on some consideration for that. For me to take this job, I'll need an advance of two hundred dollars and if I return with Sara Beth, the minimum charge will be one thousand dollars and actual expenses. If I don't come back or I come back empty handed, you're out the two hundred. In any case, if I'm still alive and I can ride, I'll report back to you. If the girl is dead, I'll let you know.'

'Seems fair. You guarantee your work or I don't pay,' Cutler said with a half smile of satisfaction.

'You got it,' Shawnee said.

Cutler rose, went to a writing table and wrote a check for Shawnee's expenses.

'Thanks. I suppose that's all for right now. If there's anything else, I'll come back and talk to you. I'll ease on over to Sidelia and talk to the law. If I have no questions, I'll get on the road.'

Cutler stood and called, 'Mary Jane, Mister Lanigan is leaving.'

Mary Jane brought Shawnee his hat and opened the front door for him. With her back to her father, she allowed Shawnee a thin sad smile. For some reason, that smile tugged at Shawnee's heart. He rode away puzzling over it.

★ ★ ★

The marshal's name was Brewster. Shawnee sat down with him in his office on Sidelia's main street.

Brewster asked, 'Well, Mister Lanigan, what can I do for you?'

26

Shawnee said, 'I've been hired to track down Hiram Cutler's daughter, the one taken by the bank robbers. I need any information you can give me about that bunch.'

Brewster smiled and said, 'Good luck in that. Chances are you won't come back with the girl, but you may be singing soprano in the church choir.'

Shawnee frowned. 'What are you talking about?'

Brewster said, 'Look, I'll tell you all I know about that bunch, which ain't much. If you still want to go after that girl, good luck to you, my friend.'

'Who's the leader of the gang,' Shawnee asked. 'I thought Cutler said something about a 'La Loba'. What kind of name is She-Wolf?'

'Pretty good name, I'd say,' Brewster chuckled. 'That gal has been known to hold down some poor bastard she caught, jerk his jeans off, grab his business, balls and all, and whack 'em off.'

Shawnee's right hand went instinctively to his crotch. 'It's a damn *woman*? I been hired to track down and shoot a woman?' he gasped.

'Sure!' Brewster laughed. 'And as far as I know, she's the meanest son of a bitch on either side of the Pecos.'

2

'You mean to tell me that a woman runs that gang?' Shawnee blurted out, wide-eyed.

Brewster laughed again. 'You don't know shit, do you? Old Cutler didn't want you to know what you was signing up to, did he? The truth is that La Loba heads up a gang of women or at least, that's what I understand. Now the way they act and think ain't like those sweet and gentle things you meet in a bar-room. One of them'd just as soon punch you in the nose or shoot off your pecker as look at you. Surely you seen a bull-dyke before.'

'Yeah, I reckon I have,' Shawnee replied, shaking his head. 'But going up against one is something I haven't done.'

Brewster chuckled. 'There's a first time for everything, but they're smart and there's seven of 'em as far as I know. When they robbed the bank here, four went into the bank and the other three went to the other end of the street and started what sounded like a gunfight. My deputy and I took off to see what was happening. That's when they pulled their robbery and got away while we were chasing ghosts at the other end of town.'

Shaking off the surprise, Shawnee asked, 'Where do you think this gang might hide out when they ain't robbing banks, kidnapping young ladies and separating fellows from their private parts?'

'I can't say for sure,' Brewster replied, getting up and going to a map of Texas on the wall. 'But it's possible they might hide up in these mountains.' He pointed to a place on the map. 'If I was goin' to hide out, I'd get me a place somewhere up in the Delaware or the Apache Mountains. It ain't no Garden of Eden, but it sure as hell would cut down on the number of visitors you get.'

Shawnee got up and went to the map. 'I see what you mean,' he said. 'There's nothing out there that anyone would have a hankering to see, is there?'

'I reckon not,' Brewster said.

Shawnee left the marshal's office and walked up the street to an office marked 'County Surveyor.' He opened the door and found a fellow sitting on a stool hunkered over a big drawing board.

'You the county surveyor?' he asked.

'You found me,' the man said.

At dawn the next morning, Shawnee loaded up Pizzaro with food and water, nudged Candy in the ribs and set out almost due west for the Delaware Mountains. In his saddlebag was a map that he hoped would guide him to where La Loba and her gang might hide from the rest of the world.

★ ★ ★

The trip west was slow and hot. Fortunately, the surveyor had been able to mark a few places on Shawnee's map where water might be found on his trip to the mountains. He cautioned Shawnee that springs come and go and not to bet his life on the next one being there. The main trail went west to El Paso but it passed too far south of Shawnee's destination so he took a more direct route, relying on the sun's track across the sky and the time of day to keep going in the right direction.

On the seventh day out Shawnee was nearing the southernmost extent of the Delaware Mountains. In the distance stood a *jacal* and scattered around it what appeared to be goats. At the back of the hut, there was a well. As he drew closer, he saw that it was indeed the isolated perch of a goat herder and, once he was near enough to the *jacal*, he called, 'Hello the house!' A man appeared in the door, gazed out at Shawnee's procession, then stepped out to meet him.

The man was scrawny, standing no more than five and a half feet, and was seemingly no more than flesh and tendons. His skin was burned dark by the sun to an almost leather-like quality. His grey matted hair hung down his back in wild disarray and a grey wiry beard hid his lower face.

As Shawnee reined Candy to a halt and dismounted, the old man asked in a voice as dry and cracked as the surrounding soil, 'What the hell are you doing ou'cheer?'

'I'm doing a little exploring for a mining company,' Shawnee lied. 'My name is Shawnee Lanigan. What's yours?'

'I'm Angus Bartleby,' the old man answered. 'You lookin' to buy some *cabrito*?'

'No, not yet, thanks, but I could use some water,' Shawnee answered.

'Water is scarce out here,' the old man said in an aggressive tone. 'I'd have to charge ye for it.'

'How much?'

'Dollar a gallon.'

'Damn!' Shawnee exclaimed. 'You

hold that stuff awful dear.'

Bartleby cackled, showing gapped teeth. 'Difference 'tween life and death ou'cheer.'

'You have a point, all right,' Shawnee said ruefully, casting his eyes across the expanse of sand, rock and scraggly brush. 'I reckon we can do business. Mind if I camp here for the night?'

'Nope, go head,' came the answer. 'Just don't try to steal nuthin'.'

Shawnee glanced at the area around the hut. 'I don't think you have to worry about that,' he said under his breath.

That evening, Shawnee took care of his animals and built a small campfire for making his coffee and heating his beans. As he pulled cans and jerky from the burro pack, Bartleby crept closer, staring at the canned goods.

'What ye got in them airtights?' Bartleby asked.

'Got some beans, some salt crackers and some peaches,' Shawnee answered.

'You got *peaches*?' the old man exclaimed.

'Sure, would you like some? I'll split 'em with you.'

Bartleby hurried back into the hut and quickly emerged with a tin plate and a spoon. Shawnee opened the peach can top with his hunting knife and ladled peach halves and a generous amount of the thick syrup into the plate. Bartelby sat down and hungrily devoured the peach slices then turned up the plate and drained what was left of the syrup.

'Damn, that was good!' the old man exclaimed.

Shawnee said, 'Well, if you like those so much, let me trade another can of 'em for all the water I need.'

'You got yourself a deal!' the old man said happily and took the proffered can into his dwelling.

When he emerged, he said, 'I'll save those for a special occasion.'

Later, Shawnee produced a bottle of whiskey from the pack and poured himself and his host stiff shots. As Bartleby became more relaxed and amiable, Shawnee ventured to find out if the old man knew anything about the all-female gang.

'Get many visitors out here?' he asked.

'They's a few,' Bartleby answered. 'Some folks come to see me when they got a hankerin' for *cabrito*.'

'Who's that,' Shawnee asked casually.

The old man cackled. 'They's a bunch of gals that live out thar,' he said, motioning to the west. 'They come by pret' regular and get a couple of kids. Pay cash money.'

Shawnee hid his excitement.

'Gals?' he said, disbelievingly. 'Living out here without men?'

Bartleby nodded his head vigorously.

'You got to be funnin' me,' Shawnee exclaimed. 'Now what would a bunch of women be doing living out here?'

The old man cackled again. 'I reckon they's hiding from the law, but they don't say so, but they damn sure wear guns on their hips. Whenever they ride in, they always want to know if anybody's been here. I don't think they trust nobody.'

'Well now, that beats me!' Shawnee said. 'Where in the world do they go from here?'

Bartleby squinted at the sky as he remembered. 'They head west from here, but I think they turn north when they pass the rise over there.' He pointed to a rise somewhere short of the mountains themselves.

Shawnee laughed. 'Next you're going to tell me that they come into your place here stark naked and do things to you.'

The old man threw back his head and laughed his cackling laugh. 'I ain't goin' to tell you that, no sir. Them gals don't like men a'tall, but they don't pay no never mind to an old buzzard like me.'

Shawnee shook his head in feigned disbelief. 'Well, if that don't beat all,' he said.

The next morning, Shawnee filled his water bags from Bartleby's well, gave the old man a can of beans as a bonus and headed west. Candy plodded on past the rise Bartleby had pointed out, then Shawnee steered her on a north easterly course that would take them along the western side of the mountains to the nearest place where he could expect to find water. As he rode, he kept swivelling around in the saddle, squinting into the distance at the hills. He had the unsettling feeling that he was being watched.

3

It was noon on the third day he'd travelled from the old goat herder's place when Shawnee spotted a patch of green at the base of the mountains and guided Candy toward it. On arriving, he was delighted to see that it really was a spring surrounded by brush, scrawny trees, and a few wild flowers. Dismounting, he scooped up a bit of the water in his palm and tasted it: it was sweet. He let the animals approach and they drank deeply.

Though it was early in the day, he decided to camp there for the night and give Candy and Pizarro a rest. In setting up camp, he saw signs of previous visitors: footprints, ash from campfires and horse droppings, all of which were days if not weeks old. After tethering the animals and setting up his camp, Shawnee walked to the edge of the brush and took a long look around. He still could not shake the uneasy feeling that he was being cold trailed, but after a half-hour of careful observation, he'd seen nothing. He returned to his camp, started a small fire and prepared his supper.

After his meagre meal, Shawnee stretched out on his bedroll and watched the sky above him darken. The night creatures were few and subdued. There was no wind to speak of. He watched Candy for a while and there were no sounds strange enough to prick up her ears. In a while, Shawnee drifted off to sleep.

He didn't know for certain what woke him. He thought perhaps it was a dream but Candy was moving her feet nervously.

Shawnee got to his feet and with his pistol drawn. He knew someone was there in the darkness, for he smelled human body odour and it wasn't his own. There was a strange pungent quality about it. He cocked the pistol and called into the darkness, 'I know you're there. Make yourself known.'

As Shawnee stood in the darkness straining his eyes for a betrayal of motion, the human scent faded and was gone. There was no answer to his challenge and he heard no sounds save those of insects that plied the night.

The rest of the night was uneventful and the animals didn't stir. When the sun rose, he made a long sweep around the outside of the spring area. He found one place in the rocky soil where a boot had left its trace. He followed a faint trail for two hundred yards from his campsite. It ended when it reached the hoof prints of a shod horse. Again he scanned the horizon in vain. He returned to his camp, refilled his water bags and canteens and loaded up the burro. After wetting down the embers of his campfire, he set out following the trail of the person he assumed had been spying on him in the night.

The trail was consistent, a single horse, travelling at a leisurely pace. He was curious to know who it was out there in that wilderness with him, the someone who had been very close but avoided contact. Late in the day, he sighted a patch of uncharacteristic green in the distance at the foot of the mountain. He reined Candy to a stop and retrieved his spyglass from the saddlebag. He stood up in the stirrups and looked long and hard through the telescope at the green area and he finally saw it, a wisp of white smoke rising from the shelter of the stunted trees and brush.

From there, the hoof print trail continued on north. He camped that night without a fire, choosing to remain invisible in the darkness rather than have hot food and coffee.

Breaking camp the next morning, he turned west and headed straight into the mountain.

Approaching the camp across the valley would be foolhardy in that he would be too easily spotted. Rather, he thought, he would work his way among the hills and ridges at the mountain's foot and approach the camp from the south side; staying among the growth of bushes and oak trees would make him virtually invisible.

In the middle of the afternoon Shawnee and his exhausted animals drew near the camp. He had managed to stay out of sight by doing a great deal of climbing, reversing his course and cautious reconnaissance, but now he was in striking range of the camp. It lay below and to the north of his position. His next challenge was to approach the camp and observe what was taking place without being discovered.

He was close enough to make out a shack among the trees below him and sunlight glinted off what looked like a pool of water. If, when he completed his reconnaissance, it was indeed La Loba's camp, then he'd have to devise a way in and out with the girl. If it was not La Loba down there in the trees, but a lonely prospector or a hermit, he would have to start his search anew.

Shawnee planned to start the downward trip during daylight, staying out of sight if at all possible. After darkness fell, he would inch his way into the edge of the camp. He made certain the animals were fed, watered and securely tethered then started downhill.

He approached the descent carefully, staying in low places, gullies and washes to remain out of sight. After sunset, he picked his way over easier terrain, but remained wary of hidden dangers. Finally he stopped. He was about forty yards from the camp and saw that there were three buildings instead of one, two cabins and one shed. A figure emerged from the larger cabin and walked to the rear. In only a minute or so, the figure returned. No one else was visible, so Shawnee moved closer. He picked his way carefully, moving a few feet, pausing for a count of fifty and moving again. Finally, he edged within a few feet of the smaller shack and he saw a spot of light emerging from a shaded window. He crept closer, pausing to listen for a footfall or any other sound of human movement, until he reached the window. He removed his hat and had started to raise his eye to the spot of light when he heard a bird whistle somewhere behind him. He froze.

What the hell kind of bird whistles like that, and at night to boot? he thought. He turned his back to the shack and peered into the darkness. The same bird called again, but from the other side of the camp. A cold sweat popped out on Shawnee's forehead. Those calls were not made by birds.

He heard someone approaching from the other side of the camp at a run and he started to move back the way he came, back to the hill. From a bush in his path not twenty feet away came the sound of a pistol hammer being cocked. A disembodied voice called, 'Hold it right there, mister, or you're coyote meat!'

He couldn't see the person talking so Shawnee stopped and raised his hands to shoulder height. Hurried footsteps came up behind him and paused. He felt a gun barrel in his back while a hand removed his Colt from its holster then slipped his knife from its sheath.

A dark figure holding a nickel-plated revolver walked out of the bush and up to Shawnee. 'Welcome, Mister Lanigan,' a woman's voice said. 'We've been expecting you.'

Shawnee thought he might as well kiss his *cojones* goodbye; the La Loba gang had set a trap, watched him approach and coolly closed the net on him. The one behind him pulled his arms down and tied them behind his back at the wrists. From the feel of it, it was a rawhide strap and it was tight.

The nickel-plated pistol wielder ordered him to turn around and walk. They walked only a short distance, to the front of the smaller shack, where his captors halted him.

'Boss,' the gun toter called, 'come see what we caught.'

The door opened and a woman carrying a lantern walked out and stood on the steps. She held the lantern up so she could see the captive's face. There was a pause then she said, 'Well, kiss my ass if it ain't sure enough Shawnee Lanigan!'

'Madam, you seem to know me. But who the hell are you?' Shawnee growled.

'Don't you recognize me, Shawnee?' the woman said sarcastically. 'You knew me well enough when you were getting in my pants.'

His captors chuckled.

The voice stirred the bud of a distant memory that suddenly blossomed in Shawnee's mind.

'Maria?' he bellowed. 'Maria O'Toole? My God! Is it you?'

'You haven't forgotten,' Maria said. 'How sweet! Now it's pay back time.'

4

From the corner of his eye, Shawnee saw other figures exiting the larger cabin and drawing near. He kept his eyes on Maria O'Toole, a girl with whom he had a steamy, noisy relationship some, how long ago was it? Fifteen years? He could see her face in the lantern light now. She was a remarkably handsome woman, not the dewy beauty that he bedded a decade and a half before but still a pleasure to behold. A pleasure, that is, if Shawnee had not felt such a tenuous relationship with his private parts at that moment. The most astounding thing was that that hot-blooded Maria he had known as a girl was now La Loba, the leader of a gang of outlaw women.

'What do you mean pay back?' Shawnee said. 'I haven't done anything to you.'

'Not for about fifteen years, you haven't,' Maria said, to the amusement of her gang.

'As I remember, you seemed to like what I did a whole lot,' Shawnee said. 'I never hurt you or was ornery to you, or beat you or anything like that.'

Maria stepped down from her front steps and walked around Shawnee, holding the lantern so she could inspect him.

'You still look pretty good, Shawnee,' she said. 'You sure as hell aren't any prettier but then you're not uglier either. You don't have a beer belly yet and you don't have turkey wattles under your chin, so I 'spose you've taken care of yourself.'

'You look pretty good yourself, Maria,' Shawnee offered. 'Danged if you aren't better looking than when you was eighteen.'

Maria chuckled. 'You were always pretty good with the snake oil, Shawnee. You never overdid it, just enough to let you get by with something.'

The woman holding the pistol on Shawnee asked, 'What are we goin' to do with this 'un, Maria?'

'Well, Alice,' Maria replied, 'I don't want to kill 'im . . . yet. I want to talk to 'im a little more before I make a decision.'

Shawnee looked at Alice and sniffed the air. 'You were the one in my camp weren't you?'

Alice's face clouded over. 'You sayin' I stink, you son of a bitch?' She raised the pistol to strike him.

'Now, Alice!' Maria interrupted. 'Don't let him rile you. He's good at that. Just take him on into my shack and sit him down. I want to talk to him before we do anything.'

Maria raised the lantern to illuminate the faces of those standing around Shawnee. 'By the way,' she said, 'this is my gang. The one you just pissed off is Alice from Dallas. The one over there with your pistol and knife in her belt is Marvalene from El Paso, that big one there is Sonoma, the short blond one is

Wynelle, and those two over there are Al and Gus.'

Shawnee nodded to each of the gang members as they were introduced. Some returned his greeting by glowering, Al and Gus both smiled. Shawnee thought Sonoma was the most threatening. She was at least six feet one inch tall and had a chin like a granite boulder. He looked closer and saw scattered black whiskers sprouting from it.

Alice from Dallas prodded Shawnee in the back and he walked up the steps into the one-room shack. Someone with long dark hair huddled in the bed. Alice turned him around and shoved him into a chair and turned to Maria.

'You goin' to be all right with him or you want me to stay?' she asked.

'I think he's tamed enough, Alice,' the gang leader replied. 'You can go on and get some rest now.'

'Reckon I need to take a bath first,' Alice remarked, turning a stony stare on Shawnee.

Shawnee spoke up. 'I didn't mean any offense, Alice sweetie,' he said. 'It's just that you smelled familiar.'

Alice fixed him with a ferocious glare. 'Don't call me sweetie,' she growled.

Maria watched the burly girl go out of the door and said, 'Alice found out about you and cold trailed you out here. Did a pretty good job, didn't she?'

'Sure as hell did,' Shawnee answered, somewhat in awe. 'I never did see her. If the breeze hadn't been blowing the right direction, I wouldn't even know anyone had been in my camp that night. I knew there was something different about that scent. It was different from a man who's been on the trail for a few days. I just couldn't figure out why.'

Maria chuckled. 'I'm surprised, Shawnee. I figured you'd be able to sniff out quim just about any place.'

Maria turned and motioned to the figure in the bed. 'Come here, honey. I want you to meet the man that came to rescue you.'

The girl threw back the covers and stepped out of the bed. Shawnee recognized her immediately. It was Sara Beth Cutler. She wore a thin night-gown. Her dark brown hair fell loosely across her shoulders and down her back. Shawnee saw that she was prettier than her photograph.

'This is Shawnee Lanigan, sweet-heart,' Maria said. 'He's the one your daddy hired to take you home.'

Sara Beth's eyes hardened. 'When are you going to kill him?' she hissed.

Maria laughed. 'All in good time,' she said. 'He's an old acquaintance of mine. I want to do some catching up before we fix him.'

Shawnee felt his testicles drawing up at the words, 'fix him'.

'Maria,' he said. 'If it's all the same to you, I rather you just shot me through the head than cut my balls off.'

Maria threw back her head and laughed heartily. 'You heard about that, did you? Don't worry, Shawnee, we did that just one time. It was a drover named Russ Welch. He raped Wynelle and beat her up 'bout two years before she came into the gang. After she came with me, she saw him standing in front of a saloon when we were in a little town, I think it was called Tawakoni Mills, and she came and told me. We caught him and fixed him so's he wouldn't be raping anyone else.'

Maria turned and looked at Sara Beth. 'Sara, honey, you want Mister Lanigan to take you back to your pappy?'

Sara Beth sneered. 'I'd cut my own throat before I'd go back to that mean old Bible thumping bastard!'

She turned and stood on her tiptoes and kissed Maria on the mouth. Maria took her in both arms and held the kiss for a long moment while Shawnee gaped in surprise. When the kiss ended, Sara Beth looked at Shawnee, saw his shock and gave him a look that could only be described as triumphant. Then she turned her back and pulled the gown off her shoulders and let it fall to her hips. In the lamplight, Shawnee saw long scars across the girl's back. It was obvious she had been beaten some time before with a whip or a quirt.

Shawnee gasped, 'Your old man did that?' When the girl nodded, he spat, 'Kiss me awake! I've been defrauded! Me! Shawnee Lanigan! But wait a minute. You knew I was coming. How in hell did you know that?'

Sara Beth said, 'Mary Ann let us know, Mister Lanigan. She told Alice about your visit to our house in Pyote and why you were there. Alice was on the way back here and stopped by to talk to Mary Ann, without my father knowing of course. You should know, Mister Lanigan, that the kidnapping wasn't real. I had met Maria weeks before in Sidelia when she was looking over the bank there. We were attracted to one another and we talked and I knew I wanted to be with her and not my father. So I arranged to be in Sidelia the day of the bank robbery and in a certain place at a certain time.'

Shawnee listened to the girl's story in amazement. When she finished, he looked at the floor and shook his head.

'I have never been so taken in my life!' he exclaimed. 'Hell, even if I hog tied you and carried you back to your old man across my saddle, you'd just up and take off again, wouldn't you?'

Sara Beth nodded and said, 'Yes.'

'All this is too much for this poor old cowboy to handle, ladies,' he said ruefully. 'Maria, if it's all the same to you, I'd appreciate it if you'd untie my hands and let me go on back home. There's no point in beating a dead horse.'

'If I do that, Shawnee, how do I know you won't bring a posse back here to kill all of us?' Maria asked.

'I wasn't hired to arrest a gang of bank robbers, Maria,' Shawnee said. 'I was hired to find and take this girl home. I can't deliver on that so I'll tell old man Cutler that I failed and couldn't find his daughter and I'll just go on home with my tail between my legs. I have no interest in pushing any farther than that.'

'Swear to me, Shawnee,' Maria said. She pulled a knife from her garments, walked over to where Shawnee sat and reached down and grabbed his crotch with her left hand. 'Swear to me, Shawnee! Swear on your balls.'

'I swear!' Shawnee replied quickly. 'I'm going to do my best to forget this whole thing.'

Maria peered deeply into Shawnee's eyes as she slowly released his vitals. 'I don't think you're lying. I think you mean it.'

'You can count on it, Maria,' he replied. 'Hell, we used to mean something to each other. I wouldn't do anything to hurt you.'

Sara Beth looked at Maria, shocked. 'You were his lover?' she asked angrily.

Maria put the knife on a table, smiled and caressed Sara Beth's cheek. 'That was a long time ago, honey, before I knew what I wanted, before I knew who I was. It was a lifetime ago.'

Sara Beth looked at Shawnee, anger flashing in her eyes. 'Get rid of him, Maria. Let him go!'

Shawnee smirked. 'Looks like your little sweetie has a jealous side, Maria. Better keep an eye on her.'

Sara Beth started to shout something but Maria grabbed her arm. 'I'll let him go. There's no need to get your ass in a stir,' she said soothingly.

Sara Beth pulled her arm away from Maria and plopped herself down on the bed in a sulk.

Maria picked up her knife again and told Shawnee to stand up and turn around. When he did, she cut through the thong that bound his wrists. While he rubbed his wrists to get the creases out, Maria yelled out the door, 'Marvalene, bring me the pistol and knife you took off Lanigan.'

In moments, Marvalene, accompanied by Alice, appeared with Shawnee's hardware.

'Give 'em back,' Maria said.

Marvalene and Alice exchanged

puzzled glances then complied.

'You lettin' this son of a bitch go?' Alice asked in bewilderment.

'No need to keep him. He's declared a truce with us,' Maria answered.

'You trust him?' Marvalene asked.

'Yes, I do. Is that a problem for you?' Maria asked.

Marvalene said nothing and took two steps back to let Shawnee out the door.

Shawnee looked at Alice and asked, 'You're one hell of a tracker, there's no doubt, but I want to ask you one thing. Did you leave that easy-to-follow trail on purpose?'

'Sure,' Alice answered with a half sneer. 'If I hadn't wanted you to follow me, you'd never know I'd been there.'

'That's what I thought,' Shawnee said with a sly grin. Then he sniffed the air twice and said, 'And you smell pretty damn good, too.'

Alice grinned broadly in spite of herself.

Shawnee turned to Maria. 'It was

nice seeing you again, Maria, or should I say La Loba?'

'It was nice seeing you too, Shawnee,' Maria said with a half smile. 'And you can still call me Maria.'

'By the way,' Shawnee added. 'Is it all right if I come by here tomorrow morning to fill up on water?'

'Sure,' She answered. 'But after that, don't come back here again or I'll have Sonoma break your arms.'

'That's enough said,' Shawnee said with a wink. He tipped his hat and stepped into the night.

Shawnee filled his water bags the next morning before the camp was stirring. As he mounted up, Alice appeared in the door of the larger shack, naked from the waist up, and waved goodbye to him. He blew her a kiss as he rode away.

5

By midday, Shawnee reached the spring where he had camped previously. He watered the animals, fed himself and grabbed a quick nap. Then he was up and back on the trail toward Pyote. He was on the trail two hours when he saw distant riders approaching. As they drew nearer, he could make out five men. They were riding directly toward him so he kept a steady pace. He reined to a stop as they approached and waved hello.

It was a rough looking bunch. One of them sported what had once been a decent nose until it got smashed. Another had a scar down the side of his face from his scalp to his jaw. They all needed a shave and a dip in clean water. They all were armed with six shooters and carried rifles in saddle scabbards.

'Howdy, fellows,' Shawnee said.

'Howdy stranger,' the leader replied. 'You out here all by your lonesome?'

'As much as I hate to admit it, that's right,' Shawnee answered with a smile. 'You fellows look like a posse.'

'Well sir, I 'spose you could say we was a huntin' party.'

Shawnee laughed. 'Game is a little scarce out here, less you're hunting horny toads or jack rabbits.'

'We're after bigger game,' the leader said. 'Name's Will Cobbett.'

He was a big, mean-looking cowboy with funny grey eyes. Shawnee noticed that those eyes made him feel like the man was looking right through him and that wasn't a good thing.

'What are you doing out here by yourself?' Cobbett asked.

'My name's Harry Jones. I'm doing some checking around for a mining company. One of those vice presidents decided there might be iron ore out here somewhere so they sent me out to take a look.'

'Find anything?'

'Nope, not a thing. I could've saved 'em the time and expense. There ain't nothin' out here worth haulin' off,' Shawnee said. 'What game you looking for?'

'You seen a gang of bull dykes out here while you were messin' around?' Cobbett asked.

'Did I hear you right?' Shawnee asked, cocking his head to one side. 'Did you say 'bull dykes'?'

'That's what I said.'

Shawnee threw back his head and laughed loudly. 'So that's what you're hunting? If you bag one, do you get it stuffed?'

The men laughed. Cobbett smiled.

'There's a gang of women supposed to be living out here somewhere. Every once in a while, they rear up and rob a bank or a store. We're lookin' for 'em.'

'Well, that just beats me,' Shawnee said, shaking his head. 'Sorry I can't help you fellows, but one thing I ain't seen is a pack of women out here. Glad

I didn't, I'd a figured I'd gone plumb loco. What you goin' to do when you find these gals?'

'We're goin' to kill 'em after we get through with 'em and take the money they got stashed. Then we won't have to worry about 'em any more.'

Shawnee forced himself to smile. 'Well, good luck to you. By the way, if you need a place to camp for the night, you can follow my tracks back to the nearest spring. There's plenty water for your horses and it's a good place to camp. It's only 'bout two hour's ride from here.'

Cobbett looked up at the sun. 'Yep, by that time, most of the daylight will be gone. I reckon we can use that camp. Much obliged to you, Mister Jones.'

'You're welcome, Mister Cobbett. You fellows have a good hunt,' Shawnee said as he rode away.

Shawnee rode straight ahead for half an hour before he turned in the saddle to look for Cobbett's gang. They were out of sight and he stopped Candy. He looked at the sun and its height above the horizon. He looked back the way he had come and he looked to the northwest, the way he would head if he were to warn Maria.

'Oh hell's fire, Shawnee,' he said out loud. 'You know you're going to warn Maria about Cobbett 'cause if you don't, it'll haunt you the rest of your life.'

He spurred Candy and they set off at a trot to the northwest. Pizzaro tugged at the lead a couple of times but gave up and fell in line.

Shawnee fell asleep in the saddle twice before the night ended. As the sun rose, they were nearing their destination. He stopped to water his two animals then pressed on toward the La Loba camp.

He was a half-mile from the trees that sheltered the camp when a lone rider emerged from the cover and rode toward him at a gallop. As the rider drew nearer, he could see it was Alice.

Shawnee reined to a stop as she

approached. She pulled up in a cloud of dust and said, 'Shawnee, what the hell are you doing back here?'

'There's some trouble heading your way,' he replied. 'I rode all night to give you a heads up.'

Alice's expression changed from one of impatience to a determined look. 'What is it?'

'He calls himself Will Cobbett,' Shawnee answered. 'He's got four of the meanest looking curly-wolves with him you ever saw, and he's looking for you gals.'

'I know the name,' Alice said, nodding. 'Let's get back to camp.'

Alice galloped on ahead while Shawnee followed as fast as he could with the burro in tow. When he arrived at the camp, the women were grouped around Maria. They all looked grim.

Maria smiled tightly at him and said, 'I thought you weren't coming back here, Shawnee.'

Shawnee slid down from his saddle, pulled off his hat and wiped his brow with a bandana. 'To tell you the truth, Maria, I didn't plan to, but when I ran into that Cobbett bunch, I knew that if they found you, you'd blame me for leading them here. I couldn't let that happen.'

'How far away are they?' Maria asked.

'I told them about the watering hole where I camped when Alice was cold-trailing me. I figure they camped there and'll set out again this morning. It's a half-day's ride from here.'

'And there're five of them?'

'Yep,' Shawnee answered, looking around at Maria's gang. 'Do you know these people?'

'Yes, I know Cobbett,' she answered with a sneer. 'A piece of trash from Caprock in Apache County. We screwed him up one time a few years ago. He's been pissed off ever since.'

'What do you mean, screwed him up?'

'We hit a company payroll over in Deep Water. Made off with a bundle, I don't mind telling you. Well, the next day, Cobbett and his bunch of slack jaws ride into Deep Water to rob the bank. They hadn't heard about us boosting that payroll and they didn't know everyone in town was carrying. Cobbett and a couple of his boys went rushing into the bank and when they said, 'This is a holdup,' about a half-dozen citizens and bank clerks drew down on them. He lost his whole gang and barely got away himself with a couple of holes in that carcass of his. He's hated me and my girls ever since.'

'That's funny, Maria,' Shawnee said, chuckling. 'So he blames you for his poor planning.'

'You nailed it, Shawnee.'

Shawnee looked at the crowd of women. 'I can't help but think he's over-estimated how good his men are.'

Maria laughed. 'Underestimated a bunch of women is more like it.'

She turned to her gang and started making assignments. 'Since we don't know when they'll come, we have to be ready starting about noon. Alice and Sonoma, I want you two up front. Marvalene, you and Wynelle watch the back approach, the one that Shawnee used the other night. Al and Gus, you two hide on opposite sides of the camp, under cover, with your rifles. If they get past the others, you'll have to pick 'em off. Everyone take a bag of water and some grub with you. There's no telling how long you're going to be waiting.'

As the girls turned to go about their business, Maria said, 'Shawnee, get your mount and your burro in the shed with the other animals, then come back to my shack. I want to talk to you.'

Shawnee unloaded the burro, but left Candy saddled and returned to Maria's shack. Sara Beth frowned at him when he walked in.

Shawnee and Maria sat at a small table. Maria leaned close and spoke softly. 'I want you to take Sara Beth and hide somewhere up in the hills until this is all over.'

'What?' Shawnee said in disbelief.

'I'm not going to run out on you.'

'No, I know you wouldn't run out, but this is what I want you to do. I can fight a lot better knowing she's out of danger. If they do manage to kill me or most of my girls, I don't want them to get their filthy hands on her.'

Maria glanced over at Sara Beth who was watching them. 'She doesn't know what a man would do to her. I can't stand the thought of her being hurt.'

Shawnee looked at the girl and nodded. 'I understand. After all, you . . . er, you have feelings for her.'

'Yes,' Maria said softly. 'If they get me, get her back home where she'll be safe.'

'Safe from getting raped, you mean,' Shawnee said, 'not safe from her pappy's whip.'

'She stood it before; she can stand it again. At least until she can make another getaway.'

'You sure you don't want me to stay and fight. I'm pretty good with a gun, you know.'

'I know you are. But what I want is to get her safe. You're the best I know to do that.'

* * *

While Maria explained things to Sara Beth, Shawnee loaded up his saddle-bags with what they would need to eat and saddled a horse for Sara Beth. He planned to spend at least one night and maybe two in the brush, well separated from the camp. He wanted to be far enough away that one of Cobbett's men didn't stumble across them while reconnoitring.

As noon approached, Shawnee helped a sullen Sara Beth into her saddle and the two set out to the north, keeping within the trees. During the ride, the girl was silent. She was unhappy over having to leave Maria and doubly unhappy over being put under the charge of Shawnee, the man her hated father hired to bring her back home.

They had travelled no more than two

miles along the rough terrain at the base of the mountains when Shawnee saw what he had been looking for. It was a large pile of rock that had fallen away from the mountain countless centuries before and rose as high as two barns stacked up. Shawnee rode around the rock, inspecting it. He dismounted and, leading his horse, walked between two boulders into a narrow defile.

Emerging from the recess, Shawnee said, 'We'll camp here.'

'Is this far enough away from the camp?' Sara Beth asked.

'Not as far as Maria wanted us to go, but far enough for my purposes. You'll be safe here and I'm close enough to help out when the shooting starts.'

'Now what do we do?' Sara Beth asked, dismounting.

'We set up our camp and wait,' Shawnee answered.

Sara Beth found a seat on a rock and watched Shawnee as he tethered the horses in the narrow defile. He explained to his ward that anyone trying to sneak in would have to go past the horses and thereby disturb the animals. He watered the horses, gathered firewood, set up a small campfire but didn't light it, then took a small branch from a tree and swept a space of level ground clean of stones for their bed rolls. He unloaded his saddlebags and took out the food he had brought. Then he lay down on his bedroll and pulled his hat over his eyes.

'What are you doing?' Sara Beth demanded.

Shawnee peered from under his hat with one eye and said, 'I'm going to get some sleep. I rode all night. I suggest you get some too. You never know when you're going to have another opportunity for some peace and quiet.'

'I'm hungry,' Sara Beth said.

'You can eat some cold beans out of a can if you want, but we can't build a fire for cooking until after dark. Can't take a chance on someone seeing the smoke in the daytime,' Shawnee grunted.

'I've got to pee,' Sara Beth said.

Shawnee peered from under his hat again and said, 'I can't help you with that.'

Sara Beth harrumphed and flounced out of the recess toward some bushes. In two minutes Shawnee was snoring peacefully.

★   ★   ★

After sundown, Shawnee awoke and started putting together a campfire. He opened a package from his saddlebags and removed a small amount of tinder. He used a flint and a piece of iron to kindle a fire in the tinder and placed it under the twigs at the base of the stack of dry sticks he had arranged.

Sara Beth asked, 'Don't you believe in matches?'

'It ain't a question of believing,' he answered. 'It's a question of trusting. I know this iron and flint ain't going to go off all by themselves like those Lucifer sticks do sometimes.'

Soon, the fire was burning and he

made coffee, opened a can of beans and set it by the fire, and unrolled a package of flour tortillas that he had brought from Maria's camp. By the time the beans were hot, Sara Beth was ravenous and ate quickly.

After supper, Sara Beth's anger had subsided and she began to get sleepy. She laid out her bedroll and got into it while Shawnee walked away from the fire and stood listening to the night noises. There was a southerly breeze and he hoped that if a battle started back at the camp, he might be able to hear the shots. He stood for a long while listening, walked over to Candy and saddled her, then returned to the dying fire and sat down.

★   ★   ★

Back at the camp, Maria walked quietly up to where Alice had hidden herself in the edge of the trees and was keeping her eyes on the eastern approach to the camp.

'Heard anything?' Maria asked.

'I thought I heard a horse whinny a while ago. It was a long way off and I couldn't be sure.'

Maria gazed out into the darkness. 'You're faster on your feet than the rest of us. Why don't you take a little stroll out there and see if you can see or hear anything?'

Alice looked pleased. 'You betcha, Boss. Let Sonoma know what I'm doing so she won't shoot me when I come back.'

Carrying her rifle, she moved almost noiselessly into the darkness. Maria walked to Sonoma's hiding place.

'Alice is going out on foot to see if she can see anything. I'll be in her place until she gets back.'

Sonoma nodded. 'If they're out there, Alice'll spot 'em.'

Maria walked back to her hiding place. Not a quarter-hour had passed when Alice reappeared. She scurried up to Maria and said, 'They're on their way, four of them. They're on foot. I figure they are going to try to surprise us in our sleep.'

Maria nodded. 'That means one may be sneaking in the back. I'll go warn the others and I've got an idea for a little surprise for these assholes. Let 'em go by and then follow. They'll figure we are in bed and try to surprise us. When they don't find us, that's when we'll kill 'em.'

Maria trotted over to Sonoma and told her the plan, then went back into the camp to tell the others.

Alice strained her eyes into the desert, trying to glimpse a movement of any kind. She glanced back at the camp and sucked in her breath. There was a light showing in the window of the girls' shack. She saw that one was showing in Maria's shack as well. She knew that the lights would be visible for some distance beyond the edge of the camp. Then, when the light in the girls' shack was extinguished, and a few moments later the one in Maria's shack went out, Alice realized what Maria was doing.

A half-hour passed and Alice heard

footsteps in the rough, rocky soil. Then she saw them, four shadows walking abreast. She crouched down out of sight and waited. When their footsteps faded, she emerged from her hiding place and waved at Sonoma. Sonoma appeared and, together, they followed the intruders.

The starlight was faint, but it was enough for Alice to see the men stop, hesitate, and split into two pairs. One pair went to the girls' shack, the other to Maria's. There was a pause, then, from Maria's shack, came a high thin whistle.

Simultaneously, the men standing at the doors of both shacks leaned back, kicked the doors open and started firing.

By the stars, it was just after midnight when Shawnee heard the battle begin. He shook Sara Beth by the shoulder and said, 'The fighting has started. You stay here, no matter what, till someone comes for you.'

6

Muzzle flashes from the doorways revealed the men firing as rapidly as possible. As the sound of the last shot died away, the men discovered their targets were not there. Sensing a trap, Corbett spun around. He saw only muzzle flashes. The sound was deafening as each of the women fired rapidly before the men had time to take cover. Corbett and his companion at Maria's shack fell immediately, riddled with bullets. One of those at the girls' shack fell immediately but the other leaped off the porch and ran into the darkness behind the shack.

Shawnee couldn't move at a full gallop because of the terrain and darkness, but he urged Candy ahead as fast as he thought she could handle. As he neared the camp, the second fusillade of shots had long since stopped. He stopped his mount, climbed down quickly, tied the reins to a bush and continued on foot. As he picked his way through the brush, there was only silence.

When he got close enough to make out the shacks, he crouched down and eased forward carefully. He saw figures moving about the camp in the darkness. He couldn't tell if they were men or women. A grunt and a gasp in the brush to his left froze him in midstride. He peered in the direction from where the sound had come. He could see nothing. He moved carefully, taking pains to be silent.

There was a cough and Shawnee saw him by the faint starlight. The man was on his knees in the brush, busy with something. From the sound, Shawnee knew he was loading the cylinder of a six-shooter. Movements of his head showed that he was glancing back toward the camp. Shawnee heard him close the pistol's cylinder. He appeared to place the weapon on the ground beside him, put his right hand to his stomach and lean forward, letting out a groan.

Shawnee heard a woman's voice. The girls were discussing going into the brush to find the one who ran away. Foolish, he thought, to go into the brush at night looking for a wounded man.

Shawnee drew his pistol and said, 'Give it up, fellow. I've got the drop on you.'

The man moved like a rattlesnake. He grabbed the pistol at his side, raised it and fired but Shawnee's shot hit him first and the slug intended for Shawnee went into the air. The man fell backward heavily and lay still. Shawnee walked over to him and kicked the pistol away from his hand. He leaned over and felt the neck for a pulse. There was one, but it was fast, thin and irregular. Then it stopped.

'What in hell is going on out there?' Maria yelled.

'It's me, Maria,' Shawnee shouted in

reply. 'The one that got away didn't get far.'

'You son of a bitch!' she shouted. 'What in hell are you doing here? Where's Sara Beth?'

Shawnee was walking toward the group of women. 'She's safe in a hiding place. Don't worry.'

'I ought to shoot your ass off right here and now,' Maria spat as Shawnee emerged from the brush. 'I told you to stay with her.'

'Well, Missy,' Shawnee exclaimed. 'I wasn't about to sit around out there in the dark while you were shooting it out with God knows what.' He tilted his head toward the place from where he had come. 'Besides, that fellow out there was waiting for you to come through that brush looking for him. He'd a got at least one of you if you had.'

'You go on back and get Sara Beth and I'll forgive you,' Maria said. 'After all, you did let us know they were coming.'

'Any of you girls hurt?' Shawnee asked.

They all answered no and Shawnee said he'd go get Sara Beth.

* * *

By the time Shawnee and Sara Beth rode back into the camp, the girls had four bodies laid out on the ground side by side.

'Only four?' Shawnee asked.

'That's all that came,' Alice said. 'We never did see the fifth one. I've sent Al and Gus out to find their horses and see if they can spot the fifth one.'

'Damn!' Shawnee exclaimed. 'Get a lantern out here and let me look at these birds.'

When Marvalene brought a lantern from the shack, Shawnee looked at the dead men one at a time. The first one was lying with his eyes partially open.

'That's Cobbett. He's got those grey eyes that look so funny,' he said with a

83

shudder. 'How about closing his eyes, by the way?'

Alice bent over the corpse and closed its eyes.

'Yeh, I remember that one and this one, too. I know which one isn't here. It's the one with a scar that goes from his hair down off his jaw. A mean-looking *hombre* if I ever saw one. My bet is that he was waiting at the back of the camp in case anybody tried to run. He probably saw what happened to his friends and got the hell out of here. The problem is he can lead others to you.'

He turned to Maria. 'Your little hideaway ain't going to be as safe anymore. If I was you, I'd move, or go after that one with the scar and kill him before he gets back to civilization.'

Maria smiled broadly. 'Why don't I just hire you to take care of that son of a bitch?'

Shawnee looked indignant. 'Maria, I do my dead level best to stay on the right side of the law. I don't hire out to outlaws, no offense, to kill people.'

'Now, Shawnee, I know you don't hire out to shoot Sunday school teachers and dry goods salesmen,' Maria said. 'But Scarface is a killer for hire who hired out to Cobbett who sure as hell was no Sunday school teacher. Since when do you have any scruples about shooting that kind of people?'

Instead of answering, Shawnee asked, 'How do you know you can trust me?'

Maria took his head in her hands and looked directly into his eyes. 'As far as trusting you goes, you could have taken Sara Beth and lit out for Pyote to collect your reward while we were waiting for these pigs, but you didn't.'

Shawnee looked sheepish. He thought a moment, the workings of his face reflecting his inner conflicts. 'I suppose you've got a point, Maria. Besides, I'm out of my fee for taking that gal of yours back to her pappy and I need to do something to keep this from being a dry run.'

Maria smiled broadly. 'I thought you'd see it my way. I can pay you five hundred for stopping Scarface, half now and half after you're done.'

Shawnee stuck out his hand. 'You got a deal.'

Maria shook his hand vigorously and said, 'You'd better get started. Scarface is scootin' across that desert out there as fast as he can.'

* * *

Shawnee headed directly for the old goat herder's place. For a traveller headed east from the mountains, the old man's goat farm was the closest where fresh water could be found. The water bags were exhausted except for one and it was getting thin. He had calculated his water usage very closely and didn't have much margin for error.

The afternoon sun was settling toward the horizon when he finally spotted Bartleby's *jacal* in the distance. He looked forward to a little conversation after three days with no one but Candy and Pizzaro to talk to. As he drew near, he called, 'hello the house' but got no response. He drew up in front of the shack and called again, 'Mister Bartleby? Is anybody home?'

There was no answer and he began to get uneasy. He scanned the horizon, hoping the old man was rounding up goats but saw no one. Then, he saw in the small corral, three dead goats. He rode toward them until he saw the blood. The goats had been shot.

He dismounted at the shack and looked inside. The old man wasn't there and things were in disarray, as if someone had picked up and thrown down everything in the shack. He walked to the water tank beside the well. There was water in the tank for the goats. Then he noticed the well's wooden cover was not in place. He walked over and peered into the well. There, at the bottom, half submerged, was Bartleby's body.

7

It took Shawnee three hours to take care of Bartleby. He used his lariat to haul the old fellow out of the well after climbing down himself and getting a loop around the body. He looked at the wounds and confirmed what he had supposed. Someone, probably Scarface, had shot the old man twice. Shawnee found a spade and dug a grave beside the *jacal*. He wrapped the body in a blanket from the old man's bed and put it under a couple of feet of soil. After that, he laid out his bedroll and got some sleep.

The next morning, he filled his water bag with water he found in the house. He filled the animals' water bags from the tank the goats had used. While he worked, he saw the tin of peaches that he had swapped to the old man for water.

'Looks like that special occasion isn't going to get here,' he said to no one in particular.

He took a sheet of notepaper from his saddlebag and wrote out a letter to leave in the house. He explained what had happened to Bartleby and why the well couldn't be used for human consumption. He signed the note and left it on the small table weighed down by the can of peaches.

*   *   *

Maria had told Shawnee that Cobbett and his family were from a place just outside Caprock in Apache County. If that community tolerated the presence of Cobbett and his gang, or perhaps even welcomed it, Shawnee reasoned that Scarface, bereft of his companions, would return there. Since Shawnee wasn't anxious to face old man Cutler back in Pyote and give him the bad news, he would try to get a lead on the surviving member of the Cobbett gang.

★ ★ ★

Shawnee arrived in Caprock dusty and tired. He was happy to see the town boasted a barbershop where they dispensed not only shaves and haircuts, but hot baths as well. Using the name Harry Jones, he got Candy and Pizzaro a comfortable stall at the blacksmith's complete with a ration of oats then, saddlebags over his shoulder, headed for the barbershop. He got his bath, changed clothes, and settled down to await a sorely needed haircut. He was glad to wait, knowing a barbershop is always one of the best places to catch up on local gossip.

He didn't have long. The customer in the chair getting a shave asked the barber if he had heard about Billy Lassiter. The barber said he had heard that Lassiter came into town by himself because all his riding companions had met with a sad fate.

The customer chuckled and asked,

'Do you know who dry gulched those boys?'

The barber answered, 'I heard it was a big gang of Comancheros.'

The customer laughed out loud. 'That's what Lassiter was telling everybody, but I heard different.'

'What's that?'

'I heard that it was a bunch of women that caught 'em, killed every damned one of 'em, 'cept Lassiter.'

'Women?' the barber repeated incredulously.

'Bull dykes. A gang of 'em. Calls themselves 'La Loba' after their leader. Understand she's about six foot six, has chin whiskers and shoulders like a man. Likes nothin' better'n cuttin' a man's private parts off and feedin' 'em to her pet wolves.'

'Damn!' the barber exclaimed. 'Hope I don't ever run up on *her*.'

Shawnee spoke up. 'Sounds like a wild tale to me, mister. Have you seen this gal?'

'Nope, ain't had the pleasure,' the

customer answered. 'Just know what I been told.'

'Who is this Lassiter fellow you mentioned?' Shawnee asked.

The barber said, 'He was a member of the Cobbett gang. He's the only one left, a real ornery son of a bitch. You'd know 'im by the scar on the left side of his face, goes all the way from his hair down off his jaw.'

'Who gave him the scar?' Shawnee asked.

'I understand it was his own mother,' the barber replied. 'The story is he was about ten or twelve when his ma decided he needed killin' and tried to cut his throat. She slashed him but didn't get his throat and he brained her with a singletree[1].'

'Damn!' Shawnee exclaimed. 'It ain't often you hear about a family as loving as that.'

The barber and his customer laughed.

---

[1] whippletree, leader-bar

'What happened after that?' Shawnee asked.

'Well,' the barber said, 'he pled self defense and the grand jury no-billed 'im. Course, it was known around the county his mother was a real heller. Since then, he's been in one kind of trouble or other. Been running with that Cobbett gang lately. Reckon as how that's over with. He'll have to find some other devilment to get into.'

Shawnee got his haircut while he listened to the barber's tales about other notorious Caprock locals. After settling up with the barber, he strolled down to the Longhorn Saloon, one of the two such resorts in Caprock. He ordered a beer and lingered long enough to learn Billy Lassiter never visited that particular saloon, having been threatened with a painful death by the owner.

Shawnee finished his beer and ambled on down to the Yellow Bird Saloon, an establishment that catered to the less reputable denizens of

Caprock, according to the people who frequented the Longhorn. The beer tasted about the same as it had at the Longhorn, and Shawnee hung around and struck up conversations with some of the locals using the Henry Jones sobriquet.

It was getting late in the day when Billy Lassiter himself put in an appearance. He walked up to the bar, got a bottle and a glass, headed to a table and sat down by himself, looking unhappy. Shawnee thought he looked even nastier than he had when first they met on the trail. No one spoke to the man and avoided his eyes.

After a decent interval, Shawnee walked over to where Lassiter sat and asked, 'Mind if I join you?'

Lassiter looked up in surprise and words formed on his lips but before he could utter them, he looked at Shawnee's face and the words stopped in his throat.

'Howdy,' Shawnee said, extending his hand. 'We met out on the trail when you was with Mister Cobbett. I was coming back and you fellows were going out.'

Recognition replaced Lassiter's scowl. 'Yeah. You were the prospector that told us where to camp. Sure, sit down.'

'Name's Henry Jones and I understand your name is Lassiter,' Shawnee went on. 'I was down at the barber shop and heard that you fellows ran into a heap of trouble after I saw you. What in hell happened?'

Lassiter looked down at the whiskey in his glass, his face grim. When he spoke, he talked in low tones so as to not be overheard by the other drinkers. 'We found them dykes that Cobbett told you about. But somebody tipped 'em off. They was ready for us, set up an ambush. Shot Cobbett and the other fellows before they knew what the hell was going on.'

'How did you get away without being killed?'

'I's watching the rear of their camp, sittin' there to shoot any of 'em that got away and tried to run for the hills. It was the middle of the night when Cobbett and the boys went in. I heard the shootin' goin' on and figured Cobbett and the boys shot 'em in their beds. The shootin' stopped for a couple of beats and then started again. I crawled on in there to see what had happened and saw all them dykes standing around, laughing over killing Cobbett and the boys. It was their six guns to my one, so I hightailed it out of there before they could find me. There warn't nothin' I could do for the boys anyway. They's all dead as salt mackerel. Just as I was pullin' out and headin' back to my horse, I heard some more shootin'. I don't know what the hell that was.'

'Damn! Sounds like you hit it lucky,' Shawnee sympathized. 'What are you going to do now?'

'I'm goin' to get even with that pack of bitches. I already told Leon Cobbett about it.'

'Leon Cobbett? That a relative of Will's?'

'Sure is. His little brother.' Lassiter leaned over the table and dropped his voice even lower. 'Leon was in gaol or he would have been with us out there. He's out now and when I told him about how his brother died, being ambushed and all, he got plumb pissed off. He's goin' to put some men together and we're goin' back out there and fix them dykes.'

'I reckon you know where to find 'em now.'

'Sure do. This time we're goin' to fix 'em good.'

'It ought to save your gang a bunch of time now that you know how to get there, and knowing where all the watering holes are.'

'Sure will.'

'Speaking of watering holes, that old geezer Bartleby was a life saver when I made my trip out there,' Shawnee said.

'Who?' Lassiter asked.

'Bartleby, the goat herder,' Shawnee explained. 'He's the old wrinkled up fellow living in that little *jacal* with the

97

sweet water well out back. Goats all over the place.'

Lassiter's face hardened and he looked away. 'Oh yeah, that old man.'

Shawnee read Lassiter's face and made his final decision. He knew Lassiter was the one who murdered Bartleby. Anyone that would kill a harmless old man needed killing himself. Knowing that made Shawnee's job easier.

8

Shawnee sat and drank with Lassiter long enough to find out he was bunking at the Cobbett place south of town. Leon Cobbettt was letting him stay there until they put a gang together to go after La Loba. Shawnee had one last drink with Lassiter and said he was going to turn in. As he left, he made a show of wishing Lassiter good luck with his hunt.

He hurried to the blacksmith's place and saddled up Candy. Going out the back way, he rode out along the south road until he found a likely place for a meeting. The waxing moon cast shadows of the trees on both sides of the road. Shawnee snuck into the shadows and waited. A pair of riders came by, not noticing Shawnee. Ten minutes later, a lone man driving a buckboard followed the riders. The buckboard had rattled out of sight when a lone rider approached from town. Uncertain whether it was Lassiter, Shawnee moved into the road to get a better look. As the rider went past the trees, he passed from shadow into moonlight. One good look told Shawnee the rider was his quarry.

As Lassiter drew near, he saw Shawnee sitting astride his horse in the road, not moving. He stopped twenty feet away and asked, 'Do I know you, friend? You waiting to talk to me or stick me up?'

'Neither,' Shawnee answered. 'I'm here to ask you about that old goat herder you killed on the trail back from La Loba's place.'

Lassiter squinted at Shawnee and recognized him as his earlier drinking companion. 'I wondered about you. What's on your mind, cowboy?'

'Why did you kill the old man?'

'Oh, is that what's eating you? Because he laughed, that's why. He thought it was funny that those dykes killed . . . Wait a minute! If you stayed on the trail, you woulda got to the old bastard's place before I did. You wouldn'ta known about the . . . '

The words stopped in Lassiter's throat. 'You! You were the one that warned them bull dykes we was coming. You doubled back and warned them. Why, you dirty son of a . . . '

Lassiter reached for his pistol but Shawnee had anticipated his action and had already drawn his Colt and fired before Lassiter could clear leather. The bullet twisted Lassiter in his saddle and he lurched. The shot and his rider's movement startled the horse and it skittered away. Lassiter almost fell from the saddle but grabbed the saddle horn and held on. Shawnee followed him and closing to within three feet, fired another round into his chest.

Lassiter dropped the reins and his pistol and sagged to the side. His left boot came out of the stirrup and he fell off the right side of his horse. The horse danced away and Shawnee sat looking down at the dying man. As he watched,

Lassiter gasped three deep gurgling breaths and after the last one, the breath left his body in a long sigh.

Shawnee glanced around to make certain there were no witnesses then spurred Candy back toward town.

*   *   *

Shawnee reasoned that there was little left to do but return to Pyote and tell old man Cutler he could not find La Loba and that he might as well consider his daughter dead. He knew the old man would prefer that story rather than the truth, which if known to him, might send him into a fit of some kind.

Shawnee had the two hundred fifty dollars that Maria had given him as down payment on Lassiter's death, so the trip wasn't a total loss. Of course, to collect the other half of the promised five hundred, he would have to make the trip back to the La Loba camp and he'd had enough traveling in that arid wilderness. He wanted to get home and relax with some amiable companionship. Shawnee spent another night in Caprock to rest himself and the animals, then set out for Pyote.

★ ★ ★

'You see, Mister Cutler, by the time I got to the La Loba camp, they were gone. You could tell by the stuff that was lying around that they had been there, oh, maybe two, three days before, but they had packed up and disappeared. The problem was trying to figure out what direction they went. Besides damn near washing me and my horse away, that rainstorm the night before I got there had washed out any tracks they may have left.'

Cutler's lips were pressed into a thin line. 'Was there no clue as to their intent, Mister Lanigan?'

'I spent an entire day going over every inch of the camp, the two shacks they lived in and the little barn where they kept the horses. There wasn't a scrap of paper, not a piece of a gimcrack, nothing that would give any scent as to where they might land next. They must have done that on purpose, burning anything that would tie to a town or a trading post or anything. So I took a long shot and went south along the edge of the Sierra Diablos, then cut across to the Apaches. Couldn't pick up a trail to save me. Of course, they could have gone north, where the ground gets higher, up toward Guadalupe Peak. But I kind of doubt it. The long and short of it, Mister Cutler, is that I came up empty. I met a few souls out there in that wilderness. Not a one of them had seen a pack of women.'

'Where do you think they might have gone?' Cutler asked, his eyes narrowing.

'If they went north, they were heading for New Mexico, but civilization is awful thin up that way; there's hardly anything worth stealing. It's more likely they headed west, cut between the Diablos and the Baylor mountains and headed toward Juarez or maybe El Paso. If they went south, they might have aimed for Fort Davis. The trouble is, all they have to do is camp out there for a few days and the best search party in the world couldn't find them. There's too much territory to cover. The truth is that I could have spent the rest of my days out there looking for them and the results might have been the same.'

Cutler stood up. 'Thank you, Mister Lanigan. Of course, I am disappointed and heartsick, but after all, you are only one man. I'll not delay you any longer. I suppose, in accordance with our original agreement, the financial matters are concluded.'

'That's correct, Mister Cutler. Sorry I couldn't produce for you. I'm going to go home now and sleep in a bed for about a week.'

Mary Jane showed Shawnee to the door but she didn't close it behind him. Instead, she gave a conspiratorial glance back at the room where her father sat and went out herself, closing the door behind her. She accompanied Shawnee to the hitching rail where Candy waited. Shawnee paused without putting his left foot in the stirrup and looked at the girl, raising his brows to indicate he was waiting for her to speak.

'How is Sara Beth, Mister Lanigan?' she asked. 'Is she well?'

'Yes, she is well,' he answered. 'And very happy. You know they were waiting for me when I got there.'

She smiled. 'Yes. I was surprised when you rode up here. I thought you would be dead.'

'I would have been,' he said, 'except I happened to be acquainted with La Loba herself. We were old friends, otherwise my bones would be bleaching out in those mountains right now.'

'How lucky for you, Mister Lanigan. Thank you and goodbye.'

Shawnee climbed into the saddle and touched the brim of his hat. 'Goodbye,' he said. Glancing back at the house, he added, 'And good luck.'

9

When Shawnee got back to his rooming house, Mrs Gunch, his landlady, was waiting for him, hand out, palm upward. Without saying a word, Shawnee reached into his wallet and produced the due rent money. Mrs Gunch counted the cash and acknowledged the payment with a satisfied grunt, then went about her business.

After seeing to his animals, Shawnee went to bed and, except for irregular intervals when he took sustenance, stayed there for three days. When he had caught up on his sleep, his strength returned and with it, that old, familiar ache. It was time for a few drinks of whiskey to stimulate his social proclivities and some amiable companionship for pleasant conversation and therapy for that ache in his loins.

On his way to the saloon, he stopped

by the county gaol for a chat with Sheriff Horn. When he walked in at the sheriff's office door, Horn looked up and laughed.

'You mean you ain't been killed yet?' the sheriff said, his eyes twinkling.

'I'm still around, been here for three days. Ain't you heard?' Shawnee replied.

'Yes, I heard,' Horn said. 'I thought I'd hoorah you a little bit. I understand you went looking for a bunch of *women*, and couldn't find 'em. What kind of a tracker are you, Lanigan, lettin' a bunch of women outsmart you?'

Shawnee grinned and sat down in the visitor's chair. 'Yep, as a matter of fact, they did outsmart me. But you don't know the whole story.'

'I know damn good and well I don't,' Horn replied. 'With you, there's always some more of the story, Shawnee. Why don't you tell me?'

'You ever heard of La Loba?'

'Yep, I have a couple of flyers on her,' Horn said, digging in his desk drawer.

'They've pulled some robberies up north of here, around Sidelia, Deep Water and places like that. She leads a pack of women who are so tough and nasty, they make the Younger gang look like limp-wristed mama's boys.'

He pulled a flyer from the stack of paper in the drawer. 'Here it is. No sketch, but from the description, she must be one hell of a gal.'

'She is,' Shawnee said.

Horn cocked one eye at him and said, 'You got a story to tell?'

'Yep, but I don't want it going any farther than right here.'

'Well, I got to hear this. So I'll take an oath it won't go no farther,' the sheriff said, holding up his right hand.

'The truth is, Sheriff, I did find those gals. In the middle of the night I snuck into their camp, hoping to find the young gal I was looking for. But they'd set a trap for me and had me cold. I was ready to kiss my *huevos* goodbye when *La Loba* herself walked up. Her name is Maria O'Toole and I knew her a bunch of years ago when we were both younger. Hell of a good looking girl and in bed, well, I don't know how to describe it.'

Horn frowned. 'I thought that bunch were all bull dykes.'

'They are,' Shawnee answered. 'Maria included. It took her a while to figure out what she really liked.'

'Hell's fire!' Horn exclaimed in horror.

'Anyway, I thought I'd reached the end of my trail, but I reckon Maria still had a soft spot for me and let me live.'

'Wasn't she afraid that you'd tip off a posse as to where they were?'

'She said they were about to break camp and move on,' Shawnee lied. 'She knew it'd take me a few days to get back to where the law was and by then, they'd be long gone. To tell you the truth, if I hadn't of known Maria all those years ago, the rest of those gals would have sliced me into hash meat and let the buzzards pick me.'

'Where did all this happen?'

'Up this side of the Delaware Mountains, way to hell and gone from anything.'

'Shawnee,' the sheriff said, shaking his head, 'you beat any damned thing I ever saw. You must be the luckiest son of a bitch in the country.'

'The angels watch over me, Sheriff,' Shawnee said with a smile.

'Angels, hell,' Horn grunted, 'more likely, Old Scratch hisself.'

* * *

Shawnee put La Loba at the back of his mind and went on about his business. His immediate business, of course, was to frolic with the soiled doves at the local bagnio where he was a great favourite. Two days and a substantial sum of money later, Shawnee had rid himself of his immediate devils and turned his thoughts back to making a living.

As it happened, two days after his chat with Sheriff Horn, Shawnee was killing time in the Horned Toad Saloon, drinking beer and swapping tall stories with Trace Chain and Wall Eye when a stranger walked in. The stranger looked around, spotted Shawnee and walked up to him.

'You Shawnee Lanigan?' he asked.

'That depends,' Shawnee answered.

'On what?' the stranger asked, frowning.

'Well sir, if you are a pissed-off husband or a bill collector, Old Shawnee just left for a vacation in Mexico.'

Trace Chain and Wall Eye leaned their heads together and chortled.

The stranger's frown changed to a mild grin.

'However,' Shawnee continued, 'if you are a lawyer here to tell him he just inherited a bunch of money from his long lost Uncle Hiram, I think we can locate him.'

'How about a job offer?'

'You just found him!' Shawnee said, sticking out his hand. 'Can I buy you a beer?'

The stranger's name was Joseph Pettingill and he represented the Double Diamond Mining Company. He and Shawnee got their beers and sat at a corner table to discuss the job.

Pettingill said, 'Double Diamond is interested in a mining location about a hundred miles from here out in Saline County. The company has learned that there are prospects of a large silver deposit and it has leased the land and acquired the mineral rights. We plan to spend some months working the mine and, if it proves out, set up a permanent operation.'

'Wait a minute,' Shawnee said, getting out of his chair. 'You got the wrong man. There's no way in hell I'm going down in a mine.'

Pettingill chuckled. 'No, you don't have to. What I'm looking to you for is security. You won't have anything to do with the mining operation itself.'

'Well, that's different,' Shawnee said, mollified, sitting back down.

Pettingill went on. 'You see, there's

been some attacks on travellers and businessmen out in that part of the state. We'll be meeting a regular payroll there and being isolated from any law enforcement, we have to supply our own protection. That's where you come in. I have five men on the payroll but I want someone who knows the country to head up the operation. I was given your name and a strong recommendation. The job is yours if you want it.'

'Who recommended me?'

'A fellow who's a friend of a company vice-president, Brick Bryson.'

Shawnee smiled and nodded. 'How long am I going to be out there?'

'At least six months. It will take that long to determine whether or not there's any sense going on with it. If we shut down, you're paid off and you come back home. If we hit pay dirt, we'll renegotiate the deal and put it on a permanent basis. To start with, we'll pay you seventy-five dollars a month and room and board.'

Shawnee frowned. 'This is kind of

different from the work I usually do,' he said. 'And in six months, I'll miss out on a lot of jobs that I would regularly do for a fee. Make it a hundred and fifty a month and you've got a deal.'

Pettingill hummed and hawed but finally agreed on a hundred a month.

Shawnee notified his landlady, stored most of his gear, packed up the rest, bought provisions for the trip and dropped in on Sheriff Horn to say goodbye and tell him where he could be found for the next six months.

'Shawnee,' the sheriff said, doubt on his face. 'You're going to be in Saline County for six months where the biggest town is Estancia with a population of maybe two hundred people? I don't believe it.'

'This could turn into a regular job, Emory. We all have to make sacrifices in a good cause,' Shawnee answered.

'Somehow, I just don't think you can last that long.'

'Why's that?'

'First, there're no whores. Second,

you can't go six months without doing something outside the law.'

Shawnee looked unhappy when the sheriff mentioned whores, but he brushed it off and forced a smile. 'You can do anything if you try hard enough.'

The sheriff laughed and waved goodbye.

★ ★ ★

When Shawnee arrived in Estancia and found it to be even worse than Horn said it was, he was crestfallen. Not only were there no whores, the only saloon in town wasn't a saloon at all, just a room off to the side of the general store where they had a plank set on two barrels. There was no beer and the liquor they stocked would gag a turkey buzzard. He decided if there were two hundred people in the town like Sheriff Horn said, a hundred and seventy-five of them were hiding. Discouraged, he rode on to the mining site.

Shawnee met the site manager, a Hiram Stoddard. The man was pleasant enough but there was something about him that put off Shawnee, a feeling the man was playing a part in a stage production. His words seemed rehearsed, even when he answered Shawnee's questions.

Double Diamond had erected temporary housing for the workers along with what they called a 'dining hall.' It was just another temporary building where there was a cook stove and long table with benches. He checked in with the site manager and was assigned a cot in one of what looked to Shawnee like a barracks. The manager told him it was the building set aside for supervisory personnel and was luxuriously appointed compared to the building where the mineworkers would sleep. Another barracks, alongside the supervisors' building, housed the supply, administrative and security workers.

The mine entrance was set into the side of one of the Barilla Mountain foothills that ranged from north to south on the west side of the camp. Company workers had already laid track from the mine entrance to the edge of an enormous arroyo where cuttings would be dumped. The company's intent was, if the mine panned out, to bring in more equipment and make provisions for a permanent dumpsite and more hospitable housing.

Over the following week, as the mineworkers were hauled in by wagon, Shawnee's four security guards showed up. Since he had not been given the privilege of hiring the guards, Shawnee had serious reservations about taking men hired for him. However, the first two who came into camp, Roger Quince and Bob Wheaten, lifted his spirits. Shawnee sized them up very quickly as competent and honest men. Quince had worked for Wells-Fargo and Wheaten had been a deputy sheriff. The next to appear was Ike Pryor, who was close-mouthed about his past and had shifty eyes. Shawnee noticed the man never looked him in the eye, but always to the side, as if Shawnee's ear were a relic and needed examining. The last to arrive was Lud Phillips. He had experience with banks and guarding payrolls. After spending time with him, Shawnee decided he was acceptable. He calculated that three good ones and one yet-to-be-seen out of four wasn't bad and he could work with that.

Shawnee learned that Double Diamond had arranged with its field employees to deposit one half of each man's pay in the bank at Fort Stockton which was the closest point reached by a railroad. The other half was conveyed from Fort Stockton to Estancia each month where it was accepted by a company official accompanied by at least three of Shawnee's men and brought back to the mine site. The arrangement was fixed for the labourers who signed on; the main reason the company gave for this was security. Since the men ate in the company mess hall, and what beer and liquor they drank was purchased from the company store, the company reasoned they didn't need much money. When they quit or the job was finished, no matter how profligate the men were with their earnings in poker games or other games of chance, they still had a nest-egg waiting for them. Stoddard's assistant, Mike Peabody, kept the pay records and could, at a moment's notice, tell any man in the camp how much money was held in his name back in the Fort Stockton bank.

Shawnee rarely saw Peabody. The man wore a ferocious moustache and a full beard so that his own mother wouldn't have recognized him. At first, Shawnee thought the man looked familiar. It was something about the eyes. After a time, Shawnee realized it wasn't the man he remembered, it was the eyes, haunted, suspicious and on guard. He had seen eyes like that before, in the faces of fugitives. Of course, even Peabody's most observant friend would not have even an approximation of an idea as to the configuration of his mouth and chin, muffled as they were beneath a luxuriant growth of facial hair.

All five of the security detail stood watch until the cash was disbursed to the individual workers. Once the pile of cash was distributed, the danger of a hold-up diminished appreciably and Shawnee's men went back to routine patrols and keeping peace in the camp. Each month, the day before the payroll was to arrive, Shawnee and either Quince or Wheaten would ride a perimeter patrol. They rode out together to a point about a mile east from the camp, then rode in opposite directions, their paths taking a circular route describing a circle around the camp to the west side where their paths met at the base of the mountains. Then they continued their courses, each roughly traversing the path just ridden by the other.

The miners had a day off once a week. Half had Saturdays off, the other half, Sundays. This kept the work going seven days a week while giving the men a day of rest. Shawnee's security men all worked on Friday and Saturday nights. When the rough-edged miners relaxed, they relaxed with a vengeance. They saved their pay for Friday and Saturdays knowing they could sleep off their hangovers the next day. Those two nights were when Shawnee and his people earned *their* pay. Predictably, those were the nights when they had to break up fights, disarm drunken knife wielders and take pistols away from their owners. Even though the workers were forbidden to bring firearms into the camp, a few managed to smuggle in pistols. During the first three weekends, Shawnee and his crew confiscated a half-dozen contraband weapons. When a smuggler got drunk enough to get into an argument, he would produce his weapon to emphasize the point he was trying to make. The smugglers all got drunk enough so that on any given weekend one of them would pull out a weapon. Fortunately, there were no fatalities, only a couple of flesh wounds and several near misses.

At the end of the first month, Shawnee was still uneasy about Ike Pryor. The man followed orders, but not enthusiastically. He appeared to move just fast enough to stay out of Shawnee's way and to put in the minimum effort to get by. But the single most unsettling thing about Pryor was that Stoddard seemed to like him. When the site boss asked for help from Shawnee, it was Pryor that he requested. Whenever a worker quit his job or was disabled so that he could no longer work, he was given a voucher for his pay and taken back into Fort Stockton by Pryor in a buckboard. There, the procedure called for the worker to collect the pay due him from the bank and go on his way. Stoddard invariably asked for Pryor to act as escort for these men, a request that Shawnee was happy to grant so his other men could be reserved for more important matters.

Shawnee dismissed his concerns and buried himself in the work he was doing. He was starting to miss the caresses of his favourite soiled doves at the Madame's place mightily and resolved to take some time off to visit Fort Stockton and explore the possibilities of that civilized settlement.

He was deep in thought on that subject one day when he was surprised by a visit from Joe Pettingill, the man who had hired him. They took time to sit down and have a drink together and Shawnee learned that Pettingill was there to take a look at the operation and report back to company management.

During a pause in the conversation, Shawnee asked, 'Where did you find Ike Pryor?'

Pettingill had a blank look on his face. 'Ike Pryor? Never heard of him.'

'You didn't hire him?'

'No, I hired Wheaton, Quince and Phillips.'

'Where did Pryor come from?'

'Beats hell out of me,' Pettingill said.

'I was authorized to hire three men and a supervisor. Oh, wait a minute! There was mention of someone that Stoddard had hired. That must have been him. I smack dab forgot about that.'

'That explains why Pryor and Stoddard are close,' Shawnee said. 'I was just wondering.'

Shawnee tried to act indifferent to the information, but his stomach warned him something was cockeyed.

10

Shawnee first heard about Stoddard's woman when two of the headman's clerks were gossiping over their lunches. Shawnee's hearing always had been particularly acute and, in this instance, served him well. The senior clerk was telling his mate about the very attractive lady who arrived late on Friday night and stayed as a guest at Stoddard's bungalow for the entire weekend. She stayed indoors, not venturing out to attract needless attention from among the woman-hungry riffraff infesting the mining camp. The clerk embellished his story to the point where the cheap assignation almost reached the heights of a royal plot. He added that her beauty was so dazzling that Stoddard was loath to let her go as the sun set on Sunday and insisted she dally with him one more night. She was finally spirited away in the wee hours of Monday morning aboard Stoddard's personal coach.

Shawnee pretended not to hear what the clerk had to say, but two days later, he was in the company store and chanced to run into Mably, Stoddard's handy man and driver.

Mably acted as driver for Stoddard's coach among his other duties. It wasn't exactly a full-blown coach, but a stripped-down version of a more luxurious stagecoach. The driver sat up front in an elevated seat. Behind his head, the coach's roof carried the baggage or cargo above the passengers' compartment, the sides of which were open. Some heavy curtains on the side could be let down to provide some relief from the elements. The rig, pulled by two horses, could carry six passengers, squeezed close together. It was commonly called a mud wagon, but Mably referred to it as a coach.

'Mably, old man,' Shawnee said, 'How about a drink on me?'

'Well now,' Mably said, smiling, 'I wouldn't be turning down a drink, would I?'

The time was mid-afternoon and the two had the store's two tables to themselves. Shawnee nursed his drink along, talked about the mine and told a funny story about disarming two drunken miners a few weeks before. He talked long enough that Mably had poured down two drinks. Shawnee poured another for Mably and broached the subject of Stoddard's woman.

'Did you get the lady back to town safely on Monday morning?'

Surprised, Mably whispered, 'How did you hear about that?'

'Old friend,' Shawnee said, 'I'm the security man. Knowing what goes on in this camp is part of my job.'

Mably was somewhat mollified. 'Oh, I suppose that's true enough. After all, when she's here, you're responsible for her safety as well.'

'You're absolutely right. I don't like to pry into anyone's business, but when it involves the camp, I sometimes have to nose around. For example, I knew when the lady arrived on Friday night, and I know when she left on Monday morning. I know she is an absolute beauty, but Stoddard never shared with me what her name is.'

Mably relaxed, assuming Shawnee was in on the plot, and eyed Shawnee's bottle. Shawnee poured him another drink. He smiled and leaned closer to Shawnee, keeping his voice to a whisper. 'Stoddard holds these things very closely, he does. But, Monday morning, when he was saying goodbye, I overheard him call her Maria.'

Shawnee's stomach did a half turn, but he recovered quickly. 'Oh yes, I remember. She has dark eyes that could suck the soul out of your body, lips that would make a man forget a new bride, lush, long hair black as a raven's wing and a body that would make a grown man weep.'

Mably's eyes grew wide. 'You know her!' he gasped.

Shawnee's stomach did another turn.

'That I do,' he said. 'But we'll keep this just between us. It wouldn't do for Stoddard to know that I knew his lady some time ago, would it? Have another drink, old friend.'

He poured two drinks and tossed his down in a single gulp, pondering the likelihood that the lady in question was his Maria. He knew there were plenty of dark-eyed *latinas* in this part of the world who sold their wares either in low dives or provided high-class services as expensive courtesans. He was letting his imagination get away from him so he had another drink and dismissed the thought.

★ ★ ★

The mining operation had been in full swing for two months and the management people were not happy. Shawnee did some more prying and learned that the earth and rocks being taken from the mine assayed out at nothing. The chemist who talked to Shawnee in confidence said, 'If you quote me, I'll deny it, but there's not enough silver in that mine to plate a dollar watch.'

'What will the company do?' Shawnee asked.

The chemist shrugged. 'They'll give it another month, but if they don't find something encouraging by then, they'll pull up stakes.'

'Why did they start mining here in the first place?' Shawnee asked.

'I really don't know. Someone sold them on this location, but I don't know who. Whoever it was won't be listened to again, I'll guarantee,' the chemist added with a wry grin.

Two weeks dragged by and Stoddard called Shawnee into his office. The headman seemed nervous and was sweating more than usual.

'I'm going into Fort Stockton to take care of some business,' he said. 'I'll need Pryor to go with me.'

'Sure thing, Mister Stoddard,' Shawnee said. 'I'll make him available. Taking your coach?'

'Yes, yes,' Stoddard answered. 'Mably, Pryor and I will be gone a couple of days. I need to exchange some information with the head office. Peabody will be in charge.'

'We'll take care of things, Mister Stoddard,' Shawnee said.

The three men left early the next morning. It was only one night later, when Wheaton had the night watch, that he woke Shawnee in the middle of the night.

'Stoddard's already back,' Wheaton said. 'He went in and woke up Peabody right away. Look's like something's up.'

Shawnee got dressed and walked over to Stoddard's bungalow. The lamps were alight and there seemed to be a frenzy of activity.

Shawnee knocked on the front door. An exhausted-looking Stoddard opened the door.

'What do you want, Lanigan?' Stoddard asked.

'I heard you were back, Mister Stoddard. I wanted to know if you need anything,' Shawnee said, glancing past Stoddard at the activity in the bungalow.

Stoddard glanced behind him, turned back to Shawnee. 'The Double Diamond people are coming into Fort Stockton for a meeting on short notice. Peabody and I will be making a presentation to them on our progress here. I don't think I'll need anything. Just make sure Pryor gets some rest and a fresh horse. We'll be going back out at first light.'

'Will do, Mister Stoddard,' Shawnee said.

He walked to the building where Mably slept. Mably had gathered up some fresh clothes and had lain on his cot to sleep. He raised up on one elbow when Shawnee walked in.

Shawnee sat on the edge of the cot and whispered, 'What happened in Fort Stockton?'

Mably glanced around at the other sleeping men, then spoke in a whisper. 'We had been there one night and the next day, Stoddard went and paid a call on Miss Maria. Peabody went to the telegraph office at the railway station and came back in a hurry. Stoddard was all excited and told me to hitch up the team. I did and we came back here like a bat out of hell.'

Shawnee nodded. 'Get some sleep. I understand you're leaving at dawn. That just gives you a couple of hours.'

Shawnee didn't sleep the rest of the night. He sat up and drank coffee until he heard Stoddard's mud wagon pull out. He stepped outside and watched the mud wagon till it disappeared from sight.

'Now,' Shawnee said to the night, 'something is about to happen and only the devil knows what.'

11

Shawnee wasn't the only person in the mining camp to be worried about what was going on. The clerical and supervisory people hastily called a meeting and asked Shawnee to go to Fort Stockton and look out for their interests. It was the afternoon of the day when Stoddard and Peabody had pulled out in haste, so Shawnee and Quince saddled up a couple of geldings from the site stable and headed for Fort Stockton.

They rode in silence, but both felt something was wrong. They pulled up in front of the Fort Stockton bank at three in the morning. The streets were almost deserted so the pair of riders went to the hotel. They roused a sleepy desk clerk and learned that Stoddard, Peabody, Mably and Pryor had not checked into the hotel. After getting their mounts fed, watered and bedded down, Shawnee and Quince got a room and snatched a few hours sleep themselves. They were up with the dawn, had their horses saddled and had eaten some breakfast by the time the bank opened.

As the doors opened, Shawnee and Quince walked in, asked for the bank president and introduced themselves as being in the security force at the Double Diamond Mine. Shawnee showed his company papers to the bank president, Mister Ramsey, and asked if he had seen Stoddard and Peabody.

'Indeed I have,' the man answered. 'They came in yesterday and told me about the mine shutting down and withdrew all the company's money. They said they had to pay off the workers.'

Shawnee spat, 'Damn it to hell!'

Ramsey looked shocked and asked, 'What is this all about?'

'Do you have any idea where they were going from here?' Shawnee asked.

'You mean they didn't go back to the mine?'

'That's what I'm saying,' Shawnee replied. 'We need to know where they have gone.'

'I have no idea!' Ramsey answered, astonished.

At that moment, four well-dressed men walked in the bank's front door. One introduced himself as Hiram Strong, Executive Vice President of the Double Diamond Mining Company. He went on to state he wanted to take a look at the local operations accounts. At those words, Ramsey paled and his knees seemed to weaken.

'My office, gentlemen,' he muttered.

Strong, his three cohorts, Shawnee and Quince all marched into the president's office. Clerks brought in more chairs. When they were seated, Ramsey mopped his brow and took a deep breath.

'As I just told Mister Lanigan here, gentlemen, Mister Stoddard and Mister Peabody withdrew all the Double Diamond funds from this establishment yesterday. They explained that the mine was shutting down and that they had to pay off the workers.'

The four company men looked at one another in wild surmise, got up and huddled in a corner talking in low tones. Strong then turned to Shawnee. 'Lanigan, what are you doing here?'

'Looking for Stoddard and Peabody. We felt like something was afoot and the supervisors and clerks voted for me to come up here and find out what was going on. What we found was that your executives cleaned out the account, including money owed to the workers, and skeedadled. I was just about to start looking for leads as to where those two fellows hightailed it to when you walked in.'

'We've got to recover that money,' Strong said, wiping his brow. 'Do you think you can find Stoddard and Peabody?' Strong asked.

'If they can be found, I'll find them,' Shawnee replied.

'Good!' Stoddard grunted. 'Recover the money and there's something in it for you. Bring back those two highbinders alive if you can. If you can't, bring back the money.'

'Where are you going now?' Shawnee asked.

'We'll speak to the local authorities and notify Houston and the Rangers. Then we'll go to the mine site,' Strong replied, handing Shawnee a card. 'This is where I can be contacted in Houston.'

Shawnee and Quince got to their feet. 'We're on our way,' Shawnee said.

Taking their leave of the worried executives, Shawnee and Quince began canvassing the citizens of Fort Stockton to see if anyone saw them leave town. They quizzed several people and finally hit pay dirt at the local stock barn. The proprietor said he had sold the fugitives a bag of oats for their horses and also helped them load four large cans of water.

He added, 'The man who looked to be in charge didn't say shit, but the mud wagon driver was a little more talkative. He asked me how far it was to Jerrytown and I told him it was about a fifty-mile ride.'

Shawnee asked one more question. 'Was there a lady with them?'

'Nope, it was just the four of them, the two well-dressed men, the mud wagon driver and the cowboy toting a gun.'

The road to Jerrytown was no more than a couple of ruts, but it was easily followed. After hurriedly loading some provisions into their saddlebags and filling two large canvas bags with water, Shawnee and Quince set out on the trail.

They had ridden at a steady pace for an hour when they saw buzzards circling a spot a mile or so ahead. They rode up to it and saw what looked like a human body lying some twenty feet off the road. The buzzards were starting to alight and inspect their next meal. Shawnee and Quince dismounted and walked over to the body. The hair was matted with dried blood and hundreds of flies were buzzing about and alighting on it.

'Oh, God!' Shawnee exclaimed. 'It's Mably!'

When they turned the body over on its back, the eyes opened and they heard a gasp.

'He's still alive!' Quince said in amazement.

Shawnee raised Mably's head and called to him. The man was deathly pale. The eyes flickered again and tried to focus on Shawnee's face. In moments, they had water to his lips and he drank greedily, choking more than once in his eagerness. After Mably satisfied his thirst, Quince took a rag from his saddlebag and washed the dirt and blood from the wounded man's face. Slowly, his confusion cleared and his eyes focused. Color began to return to his face.

Shawnee asked, 'What happened?'

Hoarsely, Mably told his story in fits and starts. 'When we left the bank, I asked Mister Stoddard what the hell was going on and said I wasn't too happy about being in on a robbery. He told me just to drive the coach and not to worry about it.'

Mably blinked his eyes and coughed. Quince gave him another sip of water. The wounded man seemed to gather his strength and continued his story.

'So I drove and we were pushing hard to get to Jerrytown. I knew that's where that woman was goin' to meet Stoddard and they was goin' to head for Mexico. Stoddard told me to stop for a minute so he could get something out of his bag. I got off to stretch my legs and I was walking around and Stoddard says to me, 'Goodbye, old fellow.' I started to ask him what he meant when I heard Pryor cock his six-shooter. I turned and looked at him and he shot me in the head.'

The old man sobbed, remembering the betrayal. 'It felt like somebody hit me with a hammer and that was the last thing I remember till I heard you talkin'.'

Shawnee looked at the wound in

Mably's head. The bullet had creased the scalp and laid it open but it had not broken the skull.

'They didn't want to split more than three ways, did they?' He looked at Quince. 'Can you get Mably back to Fort Stockton? He's got to have a doctor.'

'Sure, if he can ride double, I should be able to get him back with plenty of daylight left,' Quince answered.

'Get him doctored and settled and then come on and follow me. You know where I'm heading,' Shawnee said.

With Mably mounted on the horse and Quince in front of him, the two set out retracing their steps back to Fort Stockton. Shawnee watched them go for a moment, then mounted up and resumed his journey to the south.

To preserve his horse's stamina, Shawnee rode at an easy lope. He stopped twice to rest and water the horse and reached Jerrytown at twilight. The town, if it could be called that, amounted to four buildings huddled together on the sandy wastes; one of the buildings was a barn that also served as a stable. Shawnee rode up to the door and dismounted. A man standing by a forge looked up and nodded to him, picked up a rag to wipe his hands and said, 'What can I do for you?'

Shawnee said, 'Just some information and maybe a place to lay my head tonight.'

'Don't know about the information, but you can bunk in the loft for a night; it'll cost you twenty-five cents.'

'Did you see a mud wagon come through here with two men aboard and a third trailing on horseback?'

'Yep, sure did. Met a lady dressed in buckskin, picked her up and sailed out of here on the way to God knows where.'

'Did you know the lady?'

'Nope, a buckboard dropped her off earlier today and she waited in the shade at the store over there until that coach showed up. Hell of a looker!'

'Happen to notice the buckboard driver?'

'Got a glimpse, thought it was a woman driving, but I ain't sure. I was busy.'

'Got a stall and some oats for my mount?'

'Cost you another twenty-five cents.'

'I reckon I can stand that,' Shawnee said.

★　★　★

He had ridden an hour the next morning when he again saw buzzards circling in the air. He hoped the big ugly birds were coveting an animal carcass but his heart fell as he drew nearer and saw the mud wagon turned on its side. He slowed his mount's pace and approached the scene at a walk. He turned in his saddle, looking in all directions for any sign of an ambush. There was a hillock just beyond the mud wagon and he eyed it carefully.

The two bodies he found had started to swell and taint the air, but he recognized Stoddard and Peabody.

They both had holes in their chests. He stood up in his stirrups and surveyed the surroundings. He could see neither man nor beast on that wide expanse. He hesitated, staring at the bodies for only a moment. He had nothing with which to dig in the rocky soil and wouldn't be able to put the corpses out of the reach of scavengers, even if he were so inclined. He was about to ride away on his course when a gunshot startled him and his horse bucked then fell to its knees. Shawnee slid out of the saddle as the horse fell on its right side.

Shawnee sensed the shot was fired from the hillock and scrambled to get the horse's bulk between him and that vantage point. He lay there in the sun motionless, waiting for a challenge from his attacker. The stock of his Winchester .38–40 was showing under the horse. He managed to pull the rifle from its scabbard under the horse's right side and lever a cartridge into the chamber.

He put his hat over the end of the rifle barrel and cautiously raised it above the horse's bulk. No shot came. He raised his head and looked at the hillock. Seeing nothing, he watched for some time, but saw no hint of his assailant. After a while, he heard a series of coughs, then silence.

Taking his rifle and canteen, Shawnee crawled from behind the dead horse toward the overturned coach. As he crawled, he kept his eyes on the hillock, ready to flatten himself and fire if he saw the hint of a head appear. He reached the coach and crawled behind it, out of sight of any observer on the hillock. He glanced about through the coach. As was to be expected, there was no sign of the money. He was growing more and more confident that La Loba herself was the Maria who had been keeping company with Stoddard, gathering information on payrolls, vulnerabilities and a myriad of facts that would aid her gang in making a big score at Double Diamond's expense. It was safe to assume that Stoddard, stupefied by Maria's charms, let slip his little scheme for robbing the company and its employees and his planned decampment. If so, Maria had only to allow him to perform the felony, then pluck the spoils from his grasp at a place of her time and choosing.

Since the series of coughs earlier, Shawnee had not heard from his would-be assassin. He peered around the coach's bed, straining to catch a glimpse of the malefactor. Still seeing nothing, he crawled from behind the coach along the ground to a slight depression that would give him a modicum of cover. Still nothing. Growing bolder, Shawnee crawled several more feet until he was separated from the dead horse and the overturned coach by a substantial distance. Rising to his feet cautiously, but staying in a crouch, he worked his way around the hillock until he was able to approach it from the backside. As he approached the shooter's vantage place, he saw why he had heard nothing from the assailant. A man was lying motionless on the side of the hill.

Shawnee straightened and strode toward the body. As he drew nearer, he recognized Pryor. The man's shirt was crusted with dried blood and he appeared to be dead. Shawnee bent over him and saw that he was still breathing. He took Pryor's pistol and tossed it out of reach. He then sat beside the wounded man and raised his head, saying, 'Pryor? What happened? Can you hear me?'

Shawnee opened the canteen and poured a few drops of water on Pryor's lips. Pryor's tongue darted out at the touch of the water and his eyes opened. Shawnee poured some more water between his lips and Pryor drank thirstily and coughed. Shawnee looked at the location of the wounds in the dying man's chest and marveled that he could have lived as long as he did.

Pryor opened his eyes and stared at Shawnee. 'Lanigan! I told them you were good . . . and you found us.' A faint smile wrinkled his lips. 'We never

. . . woulda made it.'

'What happened, Pryor, was it a gang of women?'

'How'd you know?' Pryor muttered and started coughing again. Flecks of blood showed on his lips.

'I guessed it,' Shawnee said. 'I suspected that Stoddard's woman was *La Loba*.'

'You *are* good, you son of a . . . ' Pryor choked. 'She lead us right to her gang. They just . . . started shooting.' He coughed again. 'Damned Stoddard . . . followin' his pecker around . . . got us killed.' The coughing returned, wracking his body. He tried to speak again but only a gurgle came from his throat. His eyes closed and his breath started coming in rattling gasps.

Shawnee held him until the gasping stopped, then laid his head down gently.

'Your troubles are over for good, Pryor,' Shawnee said to the dead man. 'If I have to track down Maria, mine are just starting.'

12

Shawnee had no way of knowing it, but Quince had run into trouble. He got Mably back to Fort Stockton's doctor and got him patched up, but he ran into a problem in the shape of Texas Ranger Theophilus Collins. Collins was in the office of county sheriff Otis Cornblum when Hiram Strong came roaring in, his retinue trailing him. Strong wasted no time in reporting the theft of over one hundred thousand dollars and giving the sheriff a description of the malefactors. Collins, realizing the thieves would be out of Cornblum's jurisdiction in no time if they weren't already, assumed responsibility for tracking the rascals.

It was several hours after that when Quince came into town bearing the unhappy Mably to the doctor's office. Having assured himself that Mably was in good hands, Quince went to the sheriff's office to report the attempted murder and the fact that the culprits, when last seen, were heading for Jerrytown. Collins took charge of Mably and Quince for questioning. When Quince protested that he had to rejoin his partner, Collins made him understand that he, Theophilus Collins, was in charge of the case. Quince chafed, waiting for Collins to pick a direction to run in.

★　★　★

Shawnee found himself in the middle of a rarely traveled road, located firmly between nowhere and not much else, with three ripening dead men and a horse for company. He took stock and found he had enough water and food to hold on a while, at least until Quince caught up with him. In the meantime, he would gather as much information as possible.

He went through the dead men's

pockets, gathering everything, putting it in a pile in the shade of the wagon. There were coins, a pocket knife, two pieces of paper, an envelope and two empty wallets. The paper bore some pencilled notes, none of which pertained to the intended embezzlement. The envelope was from the head office in Houston. Whatever it had contained was not in evidence.

Shawnee finally gave up trying to learn anything from the dead men and climbed the knoll where Pryor had died. He mounted the knoll and, shading his eyes, peered carefully around the horizon in a three-hundred-and-sixty-degree sweep. On his third sweep, something in the distance caught his eye. It was just a speck, but it seemed to move. Was it something or just his eyes? He looked away, blinked and looked back. There it is and it is moving! He watched it until he was certain. A horse! It was a horse!

Shawnee scrambled down the side of the knoll and trotted back to his dead mount, he picked up the water bag and the canvas watering bag. So equipped, he headed in the direction of the horse. Within minutes, Shawnee realized the horse was trotting toward him. It could probably smell the water he was carrying or perhaps to the animal, a man represented food and water.

The man and the horse met there in the midst of that hostile terrain and the horse drank eagerly of the offered water. The Double Diamond insignia was marked on the inside of the horse's left ear. It was Pryor's horse and it must have fled among the gunshots when its rider fell from the saddle. When it ran itself out, the creature had found itself alone, hungry and thirsty. The *La Loba* gang had taken the coach horses, but had not troubled to go after the runaway.

Shawnee was once more on a Double Diamond horse on his way in pursuit of the Double Diamond former bank account, now in the form of cash and in the possession of Maria O'Toole and her band of *desperadas*.

The gang's trail was easy to follow and Shawnee followed it for the rest of the day. They were heading west, perhaps back to their old camp. But he could not be sure, so when the sun sank beneath the horizon, he stopped, calculating it was better to remain on the trail than assume too much and lose it in the night. He dismounted, unsaddled the horse and got it fed and watered. He built a small fire from what wood he could find, supped on the meagre provisions he had hastily gathered up in Pecos and settled down to sleep as best he could.

★   ★   ★

Quince was riding hard on Shawnee's trail. Ranger Theophilus Collins had received a telegraph message that the La Loba gang had held up a bank in Tate County and a two-part posse had been formed to pursue it. The message from his superiors ordered him to join the posse and aid in dealing with the notorious gang. By the time Collins had finished reading the message out loud to Sheriff Cornblum, Quince had put on his hat and started for the door.

Quince rode into Jerrytown and saw the blacksmith's shop. Quince jumped down and said, 'I'm looking for a man named Shawnee Lanigan who came through here looking for — '

'Lookin' for two men in a mud wagon and trailed by a fellow on horseback,' the blacksmith said.

Quince looked surprised, then grinned. 'Which way?'

The blacksmith pointed. 'South,' he replied.

'Much obliged,' Quince called as he spurred his mount and headed south.

When Quince saw the overturned coach and the dead horse he recognized as Shawnee's, his heart seemed to climb into his throat, but after looking over the scene and finding that Shawnee was not one of the three corpses lined up in the shade of the coach, he felt better.

He had to assume that Shawnee had found another mount and pressed on. Like Shawnee, he found the multiple tracks easy to follow and set out to the west.

* * *

Shawnee reined his mount to a stop and frowned at the ground. He climbed out of his saddle and bent to get a closer look at the disturbed earth. He edged the new trail a hundred feet north and stared at the multiple hoof prints. He picked out one set of prints, stepped out the distance between them, went directly back to his horse and climbed into the saddle. At that moment, he heard a distant gunshot. He turned and looked back along the way he had come and saw a lone rider approaching. He waited for the rider to draw closer so he could determine his intentions. Recognizing Quince, he smiled and relaxed.

When Quince rode up, both men

stayed in their saddles to talk. Quince explained about being held up by the Texas Ranger, the telegraph message, the bank robbery and the two posses going after *La Loba*.

When Quince mentioned the posses, Shawnee nodded. Looking a bit sick, he said, 'I knew something had spooked them.' He pointed to the trail. 'They turned on a penny to change directions from west to north. When they did, they increased their speed. Up until then, they were moving at a comfortable lope. From here on, they were moving at a gallop.'

Quince was amazed. 'You mean you have been tracking those outlaw gals? Did they get the company money?'

'That they did,' Shawnee answered. 'Their leader worked poor old Stoddard and led him right into an ambush. Then they took the money and headed home. Now, it looks like they're running for their lives. It's my guess they spotted one of those posses you were talking about.'

'What do you want to do, Shawnee?'

'We've come this far,' Shawnee replied. 'Let's press on to the end, whatever that is.'

They spurred their horses into motion and followed the trail. About four miles further on, they saw where the posse's track merged with the gang's.

Shawnee said, 'The posse and the gang must have seen each other at the same time. It took this long for the posse to close the gap. What would you say, Quince, ten or twelve riders?'

'Yes, a good number. Certainly no fewer than ten. They have the girls outnumbered.

'Wait!' Shawnee called, holding up his hand, palm open.

The two riders reined to a halt. They heard gunfire in the distance.

'They must have caught 'em,' Quince said. 'What's that up ahead?'

'That's the Coyanosa Draw,' Shawnee replied.

The two rode on at a gallop. In

minutes they topped a rise overlooking the draw. In the distance, they saw men positioned behind rocks and trees on the draw's east side, firing spasmodically across the shallow water. On the west side, puffs of smoke showed where the *La Lobas* were returning fire. On the east side, beyond where the gang was making their stand, was another group, the second posse.

The *La Loba* gang was caught in a crossfire.

As Shawnee and Quince watched, the gang's return fire slowed then stopped. In a few minutes, a white flag appeared above one of the protective rocks. The firing stopped.

It took about ten minutes for the posse to find a cloth that was white enough to qualify as a flag of truce. From the looks of it, it was someone's undershirt and its claim to whiteness was doubtful.

When the posse's flag came out, someone holding the gang's flag walked from behind the protective rocks into plain view. Even from a distance, Shawnee saw that it was Maria. She held the flag aloft and turned around slowly with her hands above her head to show that she was unarmed. The man holding the posse's flag did the same then they walked toward one another. Maria stopped short of the shallow water in the draw and the man walked through it and onto the sandy bank, stopping about ten feet from her. They stood talking for a few moments and Maria turned and walked back to her redoubt. When she re-emerged, she was leading four others, Sara Beth, Alice and Sonoma, who supported another who appeared to be badly wounded.

Shawnee spurred his mount and rode down to the meeting point.

13

Shawnee and the second posse arrived at the water's edge at the same time.

Quince looked at the new arrivals and said, 'There's Ranger Collins, the one that held me up in Fort Stockton.' Quince waved and Collins returned his greeting.

Shawnee said, 'Quince, go tell your ranger friend what happened out there and the fact that *La Loba* ended up with the Double Diamond money.'

Quince dismounted and walked over to where Collins stood.

Shawnee tied his horse to a mesquite and walked down to the water. He watched Maria and her friends wade across. Maria was pale and drawn. Clinging to her arm was Sara Beth, looking from one to another of the rough men who held their guns on the women. Alice looked sullen and wore a bloody rag on her left arm. Sonoma was half carrying Wynelle who appeared to be badly wounded in the abdomen. Shawnee assumed Marvalene, Al and Gus were dead.

Half a dozen men walked across the shallow water to the defile where the gang had fought its last battle. They returned carrying the three dead girls. One carried a large canvas bag marked with the Fort Stockton Bank's name.

Sonoma reached the near bank, let Wynelle sag to the ground and then arranged her as comfortably as possible. She removed her short jacket, folded it and put it under the wounded girl's head. Maria, Sara Beth and Sonoma then sat on the ground beside Wynelle.

'Let's string 'em up right here!' someone called from the first posse. Others in the second posse raised a chorus of voices in agreement.

A grey haired, wiry gentleman held up his hand and said, 'Let's just calm down and see what we have here, then we'll decide what to do. Some of you folks don't know me. I'm Ed Ansley. I'm the retired sheriff of Tate County. The current sheriff is lying over there. He leaned into a bullet during the gunfight before these girls gave up, so I'm taking over as leader. Anyone have any objections to that?'

Despite a few low grumbles, no one voiced objections.

'First off,' Ansley went on, 'we have to make sure the Tate County Bank's money is here.'

Two men had the moneybag and had spread the loot on a tarp on the ground. 'Here's the Tate County money,' he called. 'But there's a hell of a lot more than that in here.'

At that moment, Ranger Collins strode forward. 'Sheriff Ansley, you know me, I'm Ranger Theo Collins. The rest of that money was taken from the Fort Stockton Bank by two of the Double Diamond company executives. The gang killed them and took their money yesterday. I'm charged with taking that money back to Fort Stockton.'

'Well then, Ranger Collins, that clears that up,' Ansley said. 'How come you knew where the money was?'

'I didn't. I was ordered to break off chasing the Double Diamond robbery and join the posse chasing the *La Lobo* gang. I just found out from Mister Quince here, who is a Double Diamond employee, about the gang stealing the company money. So it was dumb luck that put me here.'

A large, rough-looking man stepped forward and confronted Ansley. 'Who the hell said you were in charge? And why the hell should we believe what this so-called Ranger says. I think we ought to get our reward out of that money right now and hang these bitches.'

Ansley looked at the man as if he were a petulant child. 'There's not going to be any talk of rewards out here. That's for a judge to decide. Besides, I've known Theo Collins for five years. He is what he says he is. Who in the hell are you anyway, mister?'

'I'm Yancy Burgoyne,' the man growled. 'And I didn't come along on this fox hunt for my health.'

Rumbles from the men behind him seemed to agree.

Shawnee eyed the bunch that seemed to back Burgoyne. They were a motley and surly lot. He wouldn't have trusted any one of them with the care of a dead horse, much less a bag of cash money and female prisoners.

Shawnee walked up to the edge of the crowd where he could see the captives clearly. Maria looked up to scan the faces around her. When she saw Shawnee, her expression changed from total despair to hope. Holding Shawnee's eyes, she tilted her head toward Sara Beth at her side. The pleading in her eyes was unmistakable; she feared for Sara Beth's life.

Shawnee nodded to her without speaking and walked up to Ansley. 'Sheriff Ansley, I'm Shawnee Lanigan and I'm in charge of security at the

Double Diamond mine. I was tracking the embezzlers that cleaned out the Fort Stockton bank account. We need to talk about the money, but there's another matter as well that needs discussion. I suggest we let the posses set up camp, bind up their wounds and get some rest while we talk.'

One of the men who had been counting the money stood up and said, 'Sheriff Ansley, I'm Will Henderson. I work for the Tate County bank. I'd like to be in on that talk.'

Ansley nodded. 'Good idea. I'd like to sit down and take stock of where we are in this thing.'

Ansley eyed the Burgoyne bunch, which were passing a whiskey bottle around. He turned to two men in the posse, calling them by name. He told them to set up a guard on the prisoners and to watch the money that Henderson was returning to the large canvas bag. He then said, 'Lanigan, Collins, Henderson, let's find a place to sit down and talk. We need to sort all this out before we push on.'

The sun was low on the horizon when Shawnee, Quince and Collins followed Ansley about a hundred feet to the mesquite tree where he had tied his horse. Ansley squatted down and waited. When the others hunkered down, he said, 'Alright, Lanigan. What is this you have to say?'

Lanigan tilted his head toward where the prisoners sat on the sand. 'One of those girls, the youngest one, is named Sara Beth Cutler. She isn't a gang member, not by choice anyway. The *La Lobo* gang kidnapped her something over four months ago during a robbery in Sidelia.'

'I heard about that,' Ansley said. 'What's your connection to her?'

'Her father up in Pyote, Hiram Cutler, retained me to find her and return her to her family. I wasn't able to do that because of some problems I won't go into here. But as far as I'm concerned, this is the chance to keep the promise I made to Cutler while he was grieving over the taking of that girl. She's only eighteen years old, she's not a bank robber and I want to take her back to her family.'

Collins spoke up. 'You looking for the reward you didn't collect before?'

Shawnee glowered at the ranger. 'There's no longer any question of a reward, Collins. I failed to get her back three months ago and I want to take her back because, by God, I made a promise, reward or no reward!'

Collins started to retort but Ansley interrupted.

'We don't need to get in a pissin' contest over this, gentlemen. So cool off!' He turned to Shawnee. 'I don't know that the men out there would understand that. As far as they are concerned, she's one of the gang.'

Shawnee looked around at the circle of men. 'Those gals out there are going to die, either here or later after a jury finishes with them, that is if you ever get them back to face a jury. Just because Sara Beth struck the fancy of

La Loba, doesn't mean she deserves to die. She's where she is through no fault of her own.'

Shawnee hoped his face didn't betray his lie.

Ansley looked thoughtful, then looked at Collins. 'Have any problem with that, Mister Texas Ranger?'

Collins looked unhappy and grumbled, 'No, I suppose not.'

Ansley looked around the circle at the other faces and said, 'That's settled then. Now let's talk about money — '

A scream interrupted his words. They looked toward the prisoners. Yancy Burgoyne had grabbed Sara Beth and was trying to drag her away as Maria clutched at her. Sonoma jumped up and covered the distance between her and the struggling girl in an instant. As she reached Burgoyne, she drew back and smashed him in the face with her fist. He lost his grip on Sara Beth and fell backward to the ground. Shawnee ran toward the mêlée. Sonoma turned to look at Sara Beth to see if she was injured. Shawnee was still running when Burgoyne, lying on the ground, pulled his pistol and fired almost point blank into Sonoma's back. The big girl fell forward on her face and lay motionless, her spine shattered.

Sara Beth began to scream. Maria jumped up and grabbed the girl, shielding her eyes from the sudden death before her.

Burgoyne got to his feet clumsily and started toward Maria and Sara Beth, his pistol still in his hand. Before he reached them, Shawnee jumped in between, his own weapon out.

'Stop right there, you son of a bitch!' Shawnee shouted.

Burgoyne started to raise his pistol but Shawnee slapped him on the left side of his face with his own pistol. The big man grunted and fell to one knee. Shawnee kicked the pistol from the kneeling man's hand and put the barrel of his forty-four to Burgoyne's forehead.

'You cowardly son of a bitch!'

Shawnee screamed. 'You just shot an unarmed *woman* in the back. What the hell kind of man are you?'

'That bitch hit me and she's a God-damn *prisoner*!' Burgoyne screamed.

Ansley reached the scene and yelled, 'What the hell is going on here?'

Burgoyne peered up at the gun barrel pressed against his forehead and said, 'You sons a bitches was dividin' up that money between you; I figured since I wasn't goin' to get no reward money, I'd just help myself to some of that young, juicy quim.'

Shawnee kicked him in the stomach. Burgoyne fell backward, groaning and holding his midsection.

Shawnee bent down, picked up Burgoyne's pistol and handed it to Ansley.

Ansley said, 'If this isn't a fine mess! What's the matter, Burgoyne, your goat run off and leave you?'

Ansley turned to the men who had been guarding the women. 'Get some rope and tie their damned hands behind them!' He turned to the men standing by Burgoyne. 'Don't let that son of a bitch have a pistol. When the time comes, I'll give his back.'

The three women left alive were huddled together, looking at Sonoma's body.

'And get those bodies buried, God damn it!' Ansley shouted. He turned to Shawnee and said, 'Let's get back to that money.'

The conferees huddled again and worked out handling of the money. At Shawnee's suggestion, Ranger Collins, Quince and Henderson would take the money and leave for Tate County. They would return the bank's money first, then Collins and Quince would move on to Fort Stockton and return the Double Diamond money. While they did that, Shawnee would take the Cutler girl and head for Pyote.

'I suggest we get to work on this right away, Sheriff,' Shawnee said grimly. 'About half those sage rats look like they're right out of the Rangers' black book.[1] They've already started drinking and I don't know how long you're going to be able to keep them under control. Right now, I'm going to talk to Sara Beth.'

Shawnee walked down to the prisoners with his canteen. The two men guarding them had tied their hands behind their backs. He held the canteen to Sara Beth's lips and she drank thirstily.

As the girl drank, Maria spoke pleadingly, 'Shawnee, are you going to get Sara Beth out of here?'

Shawnee whispered, 'I've got the go ahead from Ansley and the Ranger. If I can stay alive, I may be able to pull it off.'

He hesitated, looking at the surly men nearby. 'But I can't do anything for you, Maria.'

'I can't expect you to, Shawnee,' she replied. 'When I saw they had us caught in a trap, I knew it was over for all of us.

---

[1] Official listing of wanted men.

We would have fought till we ran out of ammunition but I wanted to keep Sara Beth alive.'

After giving Maria a drink, he let Alice drink her fill. He crawled over to Wynelle and lifted her head. She was dead.

'Wynelle's gone,' he said.

Sara Beth sobbed again and Alice said, 'She and Sonoma are the lucky ones.'

'What are they going to do with us, Shawnee?' Maria asked.

'Ansley wants to take you back for trial,' he answered. 'Whether or not he can do that is another question.'

'When are you going to get Sara Beth out of here?' Maria asked, her voice trembling.

'Right soon. We can't waste too much time. I have to get out with the others. I'll be back in a while.'

A man holding a Bible walked up in front of the prisoners. He looked at Alice.

'Have you made your peace with

God, my child?' he asked.

'Didn't need to,' Alice replied. 'He's the only man I wasn't mad at.'

The man's lips tightened. 'You are going to meet your maker soon. He loves you as his own. It's not too late to ask forgiveness, child.'

'Let me tell you somethin', holy mouth,' Alice went on. 'And you're the first man I've told this. When I's twelve years old my Uncle Roscoe got drunk and raped me! He raped a little ol' skinny twelve-year-old girl and it hurt somethin' terrible. And I'll tell you what I did. After he wore hisself out raping me and passed out from all that liquor, I snuck into his shack and I took his straight razor and I cut his damned throat. He woke up and looked at me and, before his eyes rolled up in his ugly head, he knew that was the last piece he'd ever have. So, mister Bible man, just go peddle your story somewhere's else. I got my one way ticket to hell a long time ago, courtesy of Uncle Roscoe.'

The would-be salvationist stood looking at Alice, gape-mouthed.

'I think you're wasting your time,' Shawnee said to the shocked man apologetically. 'Why don't you just move on and let these ladies alone?'

The man looked at Shawnee's eyes, nodded and walked away.

'Thanks, Shawnee,' Alice said. 'The last thing I need is a church bawler telling me where I went wrong.'

Quince and Henderson got their horses and joined Collins. Collins threw the moneybag over his shoulder and walked to his horse. He fastened the bag on to the back of his saddle and the three mounted up. They nodded to Ansley and Shawnee, spurred their mounts and headed to the northeast.

Shawnee went to where the posse had tied up the outlaws' horses. He eyed them quickly, picked out the smallest and checked the clothes in the saddlebags. He led it to where he had left his horse and tied up Sara Beth's beside it. Then he walked down to the water, filled a canvas water bag, and carried it back to load on his horse.

He rejoined Ansley and asked him, 'Do you have enough men you can trust to help you get those two women back to town for a trial?'

'I still got a couple of honest men out there. They're the ones watching the girls right now. But I can't guarantee anything. There's a few pumpkin-rollers[1] in that crowd. Burgoyne's saddle tramp friends are keeping things stirred up. Even the best man I have ain't goin' to die to keep some outlaw gal from being strung up.'

The light was almost gone when the two of them walked back down to where the women sat, their arms tied behind them. There were two campfires burning.

Shawnee said, 'Watch my back.' He squatted down behind Sara Beth, cut her bonds and whispered to her, 'We're leaving. Say goodbye.'

---

[1] Agitators, malcontents.

The girl looked at Maria with panic in her eyes. 'I'm not leaving you!' she said.

'Yes, you are,' Maria said firmly. 'They're going to hang us, or worse. The only way for you to go on living is to leave with Shawnee.'

Alice turned and said, 'Go on, honey, go while the going's good.'

Maria said, 'Shawnee will get you out of here. When you get home, then you can figure out what you want to do with the rest of your life.' Tears welled up in Maria's eyes. 'Remember, I'll always love you.'

The girl started sobbing. 'No, no, no,' she protested, struggling with Shawnee.

'What the hell is going on here?' a voice shouted. It was Burgoyne. He was wearing a pistol.

14

Ansley said, 'He's taking that girl back to her family, if it's any business of yours. And who the hell let you have another pistol?'

Burgoyne smiled a sneering smile. 'I got it and, by God, that's what counts. And Lanigan, you sorry sack of shit, you ain't takin' that little bitch nowhere.' He turned to the other posse members and roared, 'This son of a bitch is trying to get one of these dykes turned loose! We gonna let 'im?'

A chorus of protests rose from the crowd.

'You don't have any choice in the matter,' Shawnee said, releasing Sara Beth's arm and standing in front of her. 'This girl was kidnapped and I'm under contract to take her back to her family.'

'So you can collect the money we ought to have?' Burgoyne snarled.

Without waiting for an answer, he reached for his pistol.

Shawnee drew and shot the big man in his right arm. Burgoyne reeled. Ansley drew his weapon and eyed the crowd behind Burgoyne. Shawnee took the girl's arm and once again started for the horses. Burgoyne reached across his body with his left hand and grabbed his pistol. He fumbled with it to get his left hand on the grip. When he did, Shawnee shot him in the middle of his upper chest. Burgoyne dropped the pistol and staggered backward two steps. His legs buckled and he fell to his knees, wearing a surprised expression. He swayed a moment then fell forward on his face.

Shawnee didn't watch Burgoyne fall, he was already watching Burgoyne's friends. One of them, a big ugly one with a protruding lower lip, started to draw.

Shawnee turned his pistol on Big Lip and said, 'Don't try it!'

The man's arm froze. He sneered,

'I'll get you for killing Yancy, you law dog son of a bitch,' he said, his lower lip in a perpetual pout. 'It may not be today or may not be tomorrow, but I'll get your ass.'

Shawnee turned to the crowd who were watching in stunned amazement. 'Anyone else?' he asked.

Those in front of him parted and he strode to his horse, pulling the sobbing girl by her arm.

Another Burgoyne crony pulled his sidearm and started to bring it up on Shawnee's back. Ansley shot him in the left shoulder. The man fell to the ground screaming.

Shawnee and Sara Beth reached their horses and he lifted her into the saddle. Keeping his eye on the crowd, he mounted his own horse and taking the reins of Sara Beth's horse, pulled away into the night. Sara Beth kept looking back, sobbing and trying to get one last glimpse of Maria.

★   ★   ★

Shawnee knew exactly where he was going. As he and Quince had ridden toward the Draw, he had noted a place to take refuge not knowing if he would need it. Now he did need it. When Sara Beth stopped sobbing, they pulled up and Shawnee looked at her hard.

'We aren't out of danger. I know right now you don't care if you live or die, but I sure as hell care. I care about my own skin and I care about you, if for no other reason than the fact that Maria loves you and trusts me to take care of you. We are going to have to cover some ground to get to a place I know where we can camp and I can hold off some searchers if I have to. Are you up to it?'

Sara Beth looked up at him with reddened eyes. 'Yes, I'm up to it.'

He handed her the reins and said, 'Let's ride.'

They went on through the night, navigating by starlight. After two hours, Shawnee changed course and headed for an arroyo. With the girl behind him, he rode down the arroyo's shallow bank and continued for another ten minutes. The arroyo made a broad bend around a hill. After they rounded the bend, Shawnee pulled up.

'We'll camp here and get some sleep,' he said.

Sara Beth climbed down from her saddle and stood silently while Shawnee unrolled his own bedroll and laid it out.

'Get some sleep, but keep your boots on,' he told her. 'If you're hungry, I've got some jerky and two canteens full of clean water.'

He pulled a small Colt pistol from his saddlebag. 'This is a five-shot .32. Keep this with you just in case. If they kill me, save one shot for yourself. It'll be better'n letting them get their hands on you. Do you know how to use it?'

'I rode four months with Maria,' she answered, smiling. 'Of course I do.'

The girl took the pistol and concealed it in a pocket. She drank from one of the canteens and lay down on the bedroll.

'You could have been killed back there,' she said. 'Why did you agree to take me away?'

Shawnee looked thoughtful for a moment. 'I owed Maria one. She didn't have me killed when they caught me in your camp over in the mountains.'

'I haven't been very nice to you,' Sara Beth said. 'In fact; I haven't been nice to you at all. Why do you care about me?'

'I don't. Maria cared about you. There was a time when Maria was, well, she meant a lot to me, more than any woman I've known since then. It doesn't make any difference what she became or what laws she broke, I can't forget that time we had together. I did what I did for her sake.'

'They'll kill her, won't they?'

'I'm afraid so.' There was a catch in his voice. He cleared his throat and whispered, 'One way or the other.'

Sara Beth sobbed. 'You aren't as tough as you make out, are you, Mister Lanigan?'

185

'I've got to see to the horses,' Shawnee said and turned away. He watered the horses and fed them a few handfuls of oats he had in his saddlebag. When he finished, the girl had fallen asleep, so he sat down with his back to the arroyo's steep bank and dropped off to sleep himself.

The eastern horizon had just started to grow visible when Shawnee climbed up the arroyo's side. He emerged at ground evel and continued upwards to climb a small hill. As he ascended, he could hear the waters that skirted around the hillock and then cut the arroyo in their downhill course. He climbed to the hill's top and surveyed the surrounding countryside, starting at the point on his mental compass from which they had just come. He gazed patiently, turning slowly to look in all directions. He saw nothing. Finally, he climbed down the hill and, when he started down the arroyo's bank, heard Sara Beth calling out his name.

'I'm here, Sara Beth. I was just taking

a look around to see if anyone was coming.'

'Did you see anyone?'

'No. I just wanted to make sure. I figure if anyone was going to chase us, they'd start at dawn. If that's the case, we've got a few hour's head start.'

'Are we ready to go?' she asked.

'Yes. Take some of this jerky to chew on and a canteen. The only reason we'll stop is to rest and water the horses.'

She nodded. 'I've got to pee, then I'm ready.'

As they retraced their route out of the arroyo, Sara Beth started talking. 'Are you taking me back to my father?'

'Yes, I am. It's not what I want to do, it's just that I can't do anything else. Even if I was the fatherly type and wanted to keep you as my own child, I couldn't.'

'You know what he'll do to me.'

'Even if he believes it wasn't your fault?'

'Yes. He'll have to rid me of sin, drive the devil out, make me repent and save my soul.'

'I'm truly sorry,' Shawnee said. 'You'll have to find your own way out of that.'

★ ★ ★

When they reached Fort Stockton, Shawnee put Sara Beth in a hotel room, arranged for her to have a hot bath, got her fed and hired an off-duty deputy marshal to guard her while he was gone.

He left early in the morning, rode out to the mine site, collected his pay, turned in the company horse, retrieved Candy, said goodbye to his friends and wrapped up his career as supervisor of Double Diamond mine security. He returned to Fort Stockton late that night and fell into bed, exhausted.

The next morning, Shawnee took Sara Beth to breakfast, returned her to the hotel and went to the depot. He found there was a passenger train going from Fort Stockton to Pecos the next day. He bought tickets and booked his horse on the freight car. He telegraphed Silas Cutler telling him his oldest daughter was coming home and when to expect them. He then returned to the hotel and paid the deputy. After telling Sara Beth of their travel plans, he went to the stable to make arrangements for his horse to be taken to the railway station the next day.

When he returned to the hotel and started through the lobby to go to his room, a large, evil-smelling figure stepped in front of him. It was Big Lip.

'What in hell do you want?' Shawnee barked.

'I want your damned scalp,' the man replied. 'I'm going to pay you back for Yancy.'

'No need to pay me,' Shawnee said. 'I was happy to do it. Now, if you'll pardon me, I have things to do.'

Big Lip sneered grotesquely, 'The only thing you got to do is die, you son of a bitch!'

Suddenly, Shawnee's arms were pinned by someone behind him. Big Lip swung a ham-like fist and hit him in the face. Shawnee sagged to the floor, stunned. He felt hands take his pistol from its holster and drag him behind the hotel desk. He was vaguely aware of the hotel clerk lying behind the desk with blood in his hair.

The avenger bent over him. 'You left too soon, Lanigan. We took old Ansley's pistol away from him and ran off those two phildoodles he had with him. You shoulda seen what we did to them girls! They screamed and hollered a whole lot afore we finally strung 'em up, because we cut some good chunks off of 'em for souvenirs. And just so's you know, we didn't bury any of 'em. We left 'em there for the buzzards and the varmints and the worms. I just wanted you to know that.'

He turned to his companion. 'Watch him, Lenny. I'm going up after the girl, then we'll take 'em out back somewhere and do what we want to do with 'em.'

He started up the stairway.

Shawnee's head was still swimming

from the blow, but he heard what was said. He opened one eye a slit to see the man over him. An amateur, Shawnee thought, he's standing too close. Lenny was looking up the stairs where Big Lip had disappeared from sight.

Shawnee knew he couldn't wait. With his left hand, he reached up and grabbed the guard's pistol and with all his strength, he thrust his right fist upward into the man's testicles. The guard tried to fire but Shawnee had the skin between his forefinger and thumb wedged under the cocked hammer. He felt the hammer snap and bite into flesh. He yelled, 'Sara Beth! Watch out!'

Shawnee rolled and pulled the stricken guard off his feet. He thrust an elbow into the man's throat, making him release his grip on the pistol. With his left hand, he struck the guard in the back of the head with the gun's butt. He scrambled to his feet and was mounting the stairs three steps at a time when he heard a crash. He thumbed the pistol's hammer back, releasing his hand and prepared to shoot.

Big Lip kicked the door open, knocking it off its hinges and splintering the frame. As the door fell, he saw Sara Beth standing with her back to the opposite wall. He smiled, licked his lips and stalked into the room. He was vaguely aware that Sara Beth's right hand had been behind her, but suddenly came into view. Too late, he saw the pistol in her hand and the flame burst from the barrel.

The noise ripped through the corridor as Shawnee reached the landing. He ran to the open door with his heart in his throat and almost tripped over the body lying on its back in the doorway. It was Big Lip, his eyes open and his jaw gaping as if he was surprised. There was a small, round bullet hole in his forehead. Sara Beth stood against the opposite wall, the thirty-two in her hand. He leaned against the wall without speaking, relief washing over him.

Sara Beth looked at Shawnee with

her eyes glowing as if she'd seen Heaven itself. She said, 'Now I know why you gave me this,' and slipped the pistol back into a pocket.

The city marshal came to investigate, sent word to the local doctor to look at the hotel clerk and Big Lip's companion. He listened to Shawnee's story and shrugged his shoulders.

When Lenny could talk, he confessed that he and his dead companion had taken it upon themselves to track Shawnee and the girl with the objective of killing Shawnee then raping and killing the girl. When they failed to find them by trying to follow their trail across country, they calculated that they could find them in Fort Stockton.

The next day, Sara Beth dressed in the best clothes she had, which were denims and a short jacket over a cotton blouse. She had arranged her hair up on her head and when wearing her hat with a flat peak and wide brim, looked almost like a boy. Thus prepared, they departed for Pecos where Silas Cutler awaited the return of his beloved daughter to the bosom of her family. Shawnee chose not to tell her what Big Lip had sneeringly boasted to him in the hotel lobby about the fate of Maria and Alice. She had not asked about what had happened or what he thought might have happened. He assumed that her way of coping with her loss was never to ask, to see her lover in her mind's eye as she had been, still alive and beautiful.

The strange couple made the trip with very little conversation. Sara Beth sat staring out the window at the countryside but Shawnee doubted that she saw it. He disliked returning her to the place she hated so much, to abandon her to the ministrations of her salvation-obsessed father, but he had no other lawful choice. Just before they arrived in Pecos, Sara Beth leaned close to Shawnee and spoke in a soft voice.

'I want to thank you for getting me away from that posse. You didn't have to do that; it wasn't me you loved, it was Maria.' She hesitated, then said, 'Now that she's gone, I have decided what I want to do with the rest of my life.' She smiled at him, a wan, sad smile. 'You won't have to worry about me again, Mister Lanigan. Now, I'll choose my own way.'

As they pulled into the station, she peered out the window. 'There he is,' she said, her voice flat and unemotional. As the train stopped, she stood up, smoothed at the wrinkles in her denims and patted a few loose strands of hair into place. She glanced at Shawnee with a half smile then her face hardened and she set her jaw. She moved down the aisle to the end of the car and to the steps.

When they saw Sara Beth, her sisters cried out and rushed to her. They hugged and kissed joyfully. The old man waited until the initial surge of excitement was over then he clasped her shoulders, managed a thin-lipped smile and said he was relieved to have her home and thanked God for her deliverance. As the girls talked, he took Shawnee aside, took a long wallet from his inside coat pocket, removed a check from it and handed to him. It was for one thousand dollars.

'I think this satisfactorily concludes our arrangement, Mister Lanigan,' he said.

'That it does, Mister Cutler. Happy to have been of service.'

Shawnee wished Sara Beth good luck and she stood on tiptoe to kiss him on the cheek. The family climbed onto a buckboard and he watched them drive away with deep misgivings. He kept telling himself he had done the right thing. He also felt as if he had forgotten to do something but he couldn't think of what it was. He dismissed the thoughts from his mind by retrieving Candy from the stock car and saddling her up. Rather than sleep the night in Pecos, he cashed his check at the bank, bought some goods at the general store and set out on the trail for home. He kept telling himself that he had made good on a promise, but nonetheless, was ill at ease with the closing of this particular chapter in his life and the voices in his head were very bitter. His mother was unhappy with him.

Arriving back home, he managed to dismiss all negative thoughts from his mind and silence the voices by abandoning himself to a two-day frolic with his two favourites at the Garden of Earthly Delights, Judy and Norma Joyce. With his baser passions slaked, he got together with Bum McReedy, Wall-Eye Brewster and Trace-Chain Stokes for a game of poker. They drank whiskey, played cards badly and laughed long into the night.

★　★　★

A month later Shawnee walked into Flossie's place for lunch and saw Sheriff Horn sitting at a table with one of the town's prominent ladies, Mrs Elizabeth Carrington. Horn motioned for him to join them.

'Mrs Carrington, how nice to see you,' Shawnee said before sitting down. She nodded politely, maintaining a proper social distance from the notorious Shawnee Lanigan.

Shawnee looked at the sheriff and raised his eyebrows in an unspoken question.

'Shawnee,' the sheriff said. 'Mrs Carrington has been visiting her sister in Pyote and I thought you'd be interested in what happened while she was there.'

'Oh, yes, Mister Lanigan,' the lady said. 'Since you are acquainted with the people involved, I knew it would be of interest to you.'

Shawnee said, 'Well, ma'am, the only people I really know in Pyote are the Cutlers.'

'That's who it is all about,' she said ernestly, barely able to restrain herself. 'It was so tragic, so soon after his poor kidnapped daughter had returned home, too,' she said.

She immediately had Shawnee's attention.

'The sheriff reconstructed it from talking to his oldest daughter,' she went on. 'Mister Cutler, a good, God-fearing man, heard a noise outside his home in the middle of the night. He went out to investigate, armed only with a cane. You see, he didn't believe in firearms and wouldn't allow a weapon in his house.'

Mrs Carrington paused to dab at her nose with a hanky. 'He went outside after waking Sara Beth. She went to the back door and was standing there when it happened. You know he lost his wife some years ago. Tragic thing.'

'Yes, yes, Mrs Carrington,' Shawnee said impatiently. 'What happened?'

'Apparently he confronted a prowler who was armed and when he challenged the thief, the man shot him dead right there in his own yard then fled into the night!'

Shawnee's eyes widened and the muscles in his back tensed. In his mind's eye, he saw Sara Beth's eyes after she killed Big Lip.

Mrs Carrington paused to compose herself. 'It was so tragic. The three girls were inconsolable and carried on something terrible. There they are, orphaned already. Of course, Sara Beth has promised to take care of her sisters until they reach the age of legal responsibility. Thank goodness, Mister Cutler left them a home and an income so they don't have to worry about making ends meet.'

Shawnee's eyes narrowed as he remembered her words, *'Now I know why you gave me this.'*

Shawnee didn't want to ask the question, but he had to. With his throat suddenly dry, he asked, 'Did they find the killer?'

'No, they did not,' the lady replied. 'The sheriff said it was probably a transient. They could find no clue whatsoever. The only time they learned anything at all was when they retrieved the fatal bullet. It was lodged at the back of the poor man's head, just under the skin. From that, the sheriff knew the killer used a thirty-two caliber pistol. Shot the dear man in the middle of his forehead.'

Shawnee sat stunned, staring at Mrs Carrington without seeing her. He felt his breath stop in his throat. For one of the few times in his life, he was unable to think coherently.

'What's the matter Lanigan?' the sheriff asked. 'You look as if you'd just seen a ghost.'

Lanigan turned and looked at the sheriff with a blank stare. When Emory Horn frowned, Shawnee took hold of himself and said, 'That's very shocking news, Sheriff.' He got to his feet and cleared his throat. 'It's just that I seemed to be so close to the family after what the young lady and I went through. A fine, upstanding man like that getting murdered in the night . . . '

He started toward the door but stopped and turned. 'If you'll excuse me, Mrs Carrington, I appreciate the information,' he said, touching the brim of his hat. 'I think I need to talk to my minister.'

With that, Shawnee turned and left. Outside, he headed straight toward the Garden of Earthly Delights. As he strode down the boardwalk his father's voice came to him inside his head, dripping with sarcasm, 'So you forgot to get the gun back from her. Was it really accidental or did you forget it on purpose? C'mon, son, I know you. Was it because you figured the old man needed killing?'

Shawnee increased his pace and hoped Judy and Norma Joyce weren't busy.

After Shawnee hurried out the door, Mrs Carrington said, 'Poor man! I don't know I've ever seen anyone look so shocked at the death of someone who wasn't a close relative. I do hope the minister can help him.'

Sheriff Horn started to laugh but caught himself, grunted and managed to keep a straight face. 'It's alright, ma'am,' he said soothingly. 'Shawnee's a hearty soul. He'll be just fine. I'm sure he knows exactly what he needs to make it through the night.'

'Oh, thank you, Sheriff,' she said, smiling. 'I'll sleep better knowing that.'

THE END

We do hope that you have enjoyed reading this large print book.

Did you know that all of our titles are available for purchase?

We publish a wide range of high quality large print books including:
Romances, Mysteries, Classics
General Fiction
Non Fiction and Westerns

Special interest titles available in large print are:
The Little Oxford Dictionary
Music Book, Song Book
Hymn Book, Service Book

Also available from us courtesy of Oxford University Press:
Young Readers' Dictionary
(large print edition)
Young Readers' Thesaurus
(large print edition)

For further information or a free brochure, please contact us at:
Ulverscroft Large Print Books Ltd.,
The Green, Bradgate Road, Anstey,
Leicester, LE7 7FU, England.
Tel: (00 44) **0116 236 4325**
Fax: (00 44) **0116 234 0205**

LONG RIDE TO YUMA

Will Keen

Clyde Manson, a high-flyer from New York, rides from the Mexican border to Sasabe, Arizona, to rob the bank. Riding with him is Hoss Kemp and the Mexican, Guerrero. However, Manson has his own agenda . . . When they rob the bank, they leave Deputy Marshal Will Hawker shot dead, and escape across the arid Arizona deserts, chased by Marshal Slade Hawker and his posse. And during the final, bloody showdown, Deputy US Marshall Wyatt Earp makes his sinister presence felt.

TRAIL OF THE BURNED MAN

Thomas McNulty

When Rafe Morgan rides into Twisted Oak, Wyoming, he gets into a saloon brawl and horribly disfigures an outlaw named Dutch Williams. Vowing revenge, Dutch and his men take two hostages, including the marshal's daughter. Rafe joins Deputy U.S. Marshal Ethan O'Hara's posse hunting for Dutch. But with the hostages as bait, Dutch wants blood, and he wants the posse destroyed. Following the outlaw's trail, the posse find themselves in a desperate struggle for their very lives.

RENEGADE RIVER

David Bingley

Jim Bales blames the Garnett outlaws for the disappearance of his brother Hector, a federal officer. But when he wounds Charlie Garnett, his errant cousin, he finds he's no nearer the truth, the wound having caused amnesia. However, sided by Charlie, Jim repeatedly clashes with the gang. They're forced to cross the Rio Grande to Mexico, where they learn what really happened. Then, facing the final lethal clash, Charlie — his mind restored — must decide between his outlaw partners and Jim . . .

THE BRANDED MAN

J. D. Ryder

Cordy Lowell lost more than his youth when they branded him. The scar from the red-hot branding iron left him thirsting for revenge. Taking sides in a range war, Cordy found himself championing a wheelchair-bound ranch owner. His battle was against Bosewell, a greedy man who owned most of the basin, his vast wealth gained from his cattle and horse breeding operation. When the fight became personal, Cordy had a chance to find retribution — if he lived long enough.